THE WISH IN THE BOTTLE

THE WISH IN THE BOTTLE

BY MORNA MACLEOD

AN
APPLE
PAPERBACK

SCHOLASTIC INC.
New York Toronto London Auckland Sydney

ISBN 0-590-62970-0

12 11 10 9 8 7 6 5 4 3 2 1   7 8 9/9 0 1 2/0

Printed in the U.S.A.   40
First Scholastic printing, April 1997

For Ellis

THE WISH IN THE BOTTLE

1.
THE BEGINNING

LANI and Mark and Laurie had many adventures before this story begins, but none of their adventures (or " 'ventures," as Laurie would say — she was the youngest) had one bit to do with magic until the summer they spent their vacation in the cottage beside Lincoln Pond.

It all started one morning after a terrible rainstorm that had kept the children inside for two days. As a reward for being so good while being cooped up so long, Mother gave them permission to row all by themselves to the other end of the pond for a picnic.

Now, Lani, Mark, and Laurie had followed the trail through the woods around the pond many times, and they had rowed across the pond while their parents watched. But they had not rowed along its entire length all by themselves, so permission to do so now was very exciting.

The pond was part of a large nature preserve that had acres and acres of wooded hills leading up to low mountains. It was a beautiful pond, not too big, not too little. It was longer than it was wide, with a bend in the middle so that the far end, where muskrats dug burrows and played among the wild rice plants, was out of sight of the cottage. Old trees shaded the mud and rocks rimming its banks, the roots of the trees reaching out and down beneath the surface of the water to make enchanted stairsteps when climbing out of the rowboat.

Lani, who was the oldest and very responsible, made a lunch of peanut butter and jelly sandwiches on soft white bread. Though the rowboat was quite safe and not at all leaky, the thunderstorm had filled it with rainwater, so Mark set about bailing it out and then put the oars in the oarlocks. Laurie raced upstairs to get her lion doll (it roared when you pulled a string on its back) and tied a bright red ribbon about its neck.

There was a bit of a fuss as the children stood beside the rowboat putting on their orange life jackets.

"You can't bring Lion," Mark stated flatly. "This trip is not for dolls." He was bringing Father's binoculars so he could watch birds. If Laurie pulled Lion's string at the wrong moment, the roar would scare the birds away.

"It's not a doll, it's an animal." Laurie hugged Lion

tightly against her life jacket. "And you can't tell me what to do."

"She could leave it in the boat while we eat, Mark," Lani suggested with an anxious glance toward the back porch where Mother had set up her easel. An argument now between the younger two might change Mother's mind about their expedition. "You won't be bird-watching while we're rowing."

"What's this 'we' stuff? I'm the captain of this boat. You're the cook. I'm doing all the rowing."

Mother peered around the easel and called, "Mark will row to the picnic area. Lani will row back. And Laurie, if Lion gets wet or even a little damp, you won't be permitted to take him to bed with you tonight." She smiled that gentle but firm smile that meant no argument.

"I know," Laurie said brightly, "I'll leave Lion on the dock to watch and make sure the big turtles don't get us."

Lani grinned with relief. "Good idea, Laurie."

Indeed, there were big turtles in the pond, some with shells as wide as eighteen inches. Warned by Father — he was a biology teacher — the children avoided wading in the shallows. After all, there was no telling how mad a turtle resting in the mud might become if it was stepped on.

Knowing there were giant turtles lurking somewhere

beneath the murky surface made rowing the length of the pond by themselves all the more adventuresome for the children.

Mark stood very straight, his life jacket puffed out, and announced, "All aboard. This boat departs in one minute."

Laurie quickly arranged Lion on the dock, where he could look out over the pond, then scrambled down into the rowboat. She chose to sit on the little triangular board in the prow, where the front sides of the boat came together. Lani sat aft, at the back of the boat, with the picnic bag and a thermos of milk next to her. Besides Father's binoculars, which hung about Mark's neck on a leather strap, Mark brought his insect net; he collected butterflies. Lani offered to hold the net while he rowed, and Mark settled upon the center seat.

Mother stepped down from the porch and, holding her paintbrush between her teeth, she knelt and untied the rowboat and pushed it away from the dock.

Father came out from the barn, which had an office where he could write undisturbed, and waved and shouted, "Be careful. Don't stand up," which the children already knew not to do in a boat or canoe, but reminders never hurt.

Mark had a few awkward moments until he managed to get both oars pulling at the same time. Then, cheered by Mother and Father, he got control and rowed out toward the center of the pond. The insect

net, which Lani held over her shoulder, streamed out behind like a ship's banner.

"Let's sing a sea chantey," Lani suggested.

"What's that?" Laurie asked.

"A song sailors sing," Mark said. "I don't know any."

" 'Yo-ho-ho and a bottle of rum,' " Lani chanted in her deepest voice. Then in her normal voice, "That's all I know."

So the three children chanted "Yo-ho-ho and a bottle of rum" over and over.

There was a light wind blowing, and tiny wavelets smacked against the sides of the boat until Mark rowed around the bend in the pond. The water there was protected from the wind by the woods, and the surface of the pond was calm and quiet.

Laurie said, "I'll look for turtles," and leaned over the side to watch her reflection.

Mark glanced over his shoulder to get his bearings, then headed the rowboat toward an old hemlock leaning out over the water. A twisty little stream joined the pond close by the tree, and along its borders were thick growths of fern. It was an inviting lunch spot, and the girls were pleased with Mark's choice of a landing.

They took off their life jackets and sprawled beneath the tree. Lani handed out sandwiches and paper cups of milk poured from the thermos. The food tasted quite delicious, as it always does when eaten away from the table.

It was a drowsy time of day, so all three were content to sit quietly as they ate. They watched the birds above them and the muskrats moving among the wild rice plants. Beyond the end of the pond, deep in the woods, a sudden drumming noise echoed.

Mark identified the sound. "Pileated woodpecker."

The girls nodded. They all knew a lot about birds, but Mark was the authority. He was always reading books about birds and other animals, while Lani liked to read science fiction. Laurie was not much of a reader, but she enjoyed looking through picture books of princes and princesses and castles and dragons.

"Oh, look!" Laurie pointed above.

A huge bird came floating over the tops of the pines, its long legs drifting behind it.

Mark whispered, "It's a great blue heron. Everybody, be still. It doesn't see us."

"Give me the binoculars, Mark," Laurie said.

"No! Nobody's moving! And, Laurie, if you scare it away — Don't move! I think it's going to land."

"But I can't see," Laurie complained.

"You have eyes the same as us," hissed Lani.

Of course this was true. But Laurie, being the youngest, felt she couldn't possibly see as much as the others.

The great blue heron made a lazy circle over the end of the pond, drifting down toward the shallows where the wild rice grew. Its wings curved to cup the air at the same time its long legs reached forward, and it landed almost without a splash no more than thirty yards from where the three motionless children watched from beneath the pine tree.

For the longest time, a very long time for Laurie, the fascinated children lay quite still, their eyes riveted on the big bird as its head tilted from one side to the other, its eyes searching the shallow water washing over its feet.

"What's it doing?" Laurie whispered.

"Looking for a frog," Lani answered in a low voice.

"Be quiet, you two," Mark growled. "You'll scare it away."

With a suddenness that made the children blink and jump a bit, the heron's beak plunged into the pond. Just as quickly, its head jerked back. Grasped sidewise in its bill was the frantically struggling body of a small fish.

"Yuk!" whispered Laurie.

Lifting its feet high, the tall bird walked through the shallows to a sloping rock and stepped up upon it. It turned its head from side to side. And while it checked its surroundings to make certain it was safely alone, the little fish squirmed and squirmed.

Laurie sucked in her cheeks and looked squeamish. She flopped over on her back to stare up through the overhanging branches at the blue sky.

Mark's first thought was to give a good punch at

Laurie for moving about when everybody was supposed to stay quiet and not scare off the heron, but it *was* rather nasty to watch one animal prepare to eat another.

Lani said in a whisper, "Laurie, if you don't want to watch the heron feed, you don't have to. But lie still."

"It's going to eat the fish and it's still alive!"

"Shhhh!" Mark hissed.

Ignoring both her brother and sister, Laurie rolled onto her hands and knees and began to crawl away.

"Laurie!" Mark threatened between his teeth as he glanced back and forth between the heron and his retreating younger sister.

Fortunately, the heron was now intent on making its meal and Laurie's movements went unnoticed. With a series of rapid head jerks, the heron skewed the fish about until it was lined up with its gullet. Then with an upward stretch of its neck, it swallowed the little fish.

The long, graceful neck of the bird now looked pretty silly with a fish bulging inside. Lani and Mark covered their mouths with their hands to muffle their giggles.

While all this was going on, Laurie had snatched away Mark's butterfly net and crawled back under the ferns. She continued on some yards, dragging the net with her, until she could not see the pond when she looked over her shoulder. She lay down flat on her back and pulled the net across her chest. She smiled. It was quite pleasant to be nestled about by frilly ferns and to have them arching above her head — they created the feeling of being in a green cave. The ground beneath her was soft and gave off a sweet, moist earthy smell.

As Laurie took a deep breath, she arched her neck back and saw a butterfly hanging from a fern frond just beyond the top of her head.

It was a unique-looking butterfly. The wings, which were about two inches long, shimmered with light although they were not moving and there was no sunshine touching them. It was almost as if there were a tiny lightbulb tucked inside its wings, a light that made Laurie want to touch it.

She stared at the butterfly until her neck began to ache. She was wishing she could somehow catch it, when her fingers tightened upon the metal rim of the butterfly net that was lying across her chest. Holding her breath, she slowly inched the net past her face until it was right beneath the butterfly. Then, with a darting upward thrust and a quick twist of the handle, she trapped the insect.

"Mark . . . *Mark!*" she whispered loudly. "I caught a butterfly!"

"What color are the wings?" Mark's voice hissed back at her from beside the pond. He was, after all, a butterfly collector, and he was too curious not to want to know more.

"Sort of whitey yellow."

"A sulphur," Mark pronounced in a disinterested whisper. Suddenly suspicious, his eyes searched the ground. "You *caught* . . . ? Laurie, you took my net!" he said loudly.

Even from back in the fronds, Laurie could hear the whoosh of wings as the startled heron took off at the sound of Mark's angry voice.

"Uh-huh!" Laurie said to herself.

"Now look what you've done, Mark," Lani accused, her voice as loud as Mark's.

"I didn't do it," Mark defended himself. "Laurie did. She took my net!"

"There it goes," Lani said wistfully.

There were moments of silence while the two older children watched the great blue heron slowly climb and then skim away over the tops of the far pines.

Clutching the net, Laurie jumped to her feet and ran off through the ferns. She knew she should stay with the other two, but she didn't want to go back to them and have to hand over Mark's net; not when she had a big, gorgeous butterfly inside that she had caught all by herself. It might get loose.

"Laurie!" Lani yelled after her. "You come back here! You're supposed to stay with us. I'm going to tell Mother."

"And I'm going to tell her you took my net!" Mark's voice echoed through the woods.

In no time, Laurie came upon the trail around the pond, and she was skipping down it toward the cottage. And in no time, Lani and Mark had cleaned up the picnic spot and Lani was rowing as fast as she could down the length of the pond.

Although Father and Mother encouraged them to go exploring, they firmly insisted that the three children stay together and not get separated. So now Lani — who, remember, was very responsible — was feeling somehow at fault that Laurie had struck out for home by herself. And, of course, Mark was angry about his net.

With her head start, Laurie arrived back at the cottage long before the rowboat carrying Lani and Mark reached the dock.

"There she is with my net!" Mark cried, peering past Lani to see Laurie on the edge of the porch. "Row faster!"

"I'm going," Lani puffed as she pulled back on the oars, "as fast as I can. Don't get so excited. As far as we know, she hasn't damaged it or anything."

The thought of a tear in his net had not occurred to Mark. His face turned an angry pink and his eyes watered. "If she's put a hole in it, I'll — I'll . . ." His mouth worked frantically, but the fiendish thoughts of what he'd do to Laurie were too overwhelming for speech.

"Don't you dare start a fight, Mark. If They — "

"They" always referred to Mother and Father. "If They hear, we won't get to go to the movies tonight."

It was Friday, and every Friday night the family drove to the drive-in theater in Greenville for a movie and a junk food dinner of hot dogs and popcorn and something cold and fizzy. Lani knew that a noisy quarrel between the younger two might result in none of them going to the movies, a possibility that was almost too awful to think about.

"I didn't start it, she did!"

Laurie saw Mother walking across the lawn to the barn. But Mother did not see her, so Laurie quickly made her way past the easel, across the porch, and inside to the kitchen. Finding an empty bottle in the cupboard below the sink, she slid it inside Mark's net and shook the butterfly, whose wings were now tightly folded, into the jar, and capped it.

The instant the rowboat touched the dock, Mark scrambled up onto its rough planking.

"Mark!" Lani warned, hurriedly winding the boat's rope around a piling. She raced after him.

Mark called over his shoulder, "It's my net. She had no right to use it without my permission." He ran into the cottage and up the stairs.

Lani was right behind him, and when he reached the tiny landing, she managed to catch him around one calf. His shoe thudded into her shoulder, but she hung on. With a tug and a grunt she pulled him into a heap on the steps. She said breathlessly, "Just don't make her cry. Promise me that."

Mark quietly struggled, putting all his energy into freeing his legs, for Lani now had a good grasp on both of them. But she was bigger than he and he could not get loose.

"Let go!"

"Promise you won't make her cry," Lani insisted.

Mark glared at her. It was very difficult being the only boy and having one sister younger, whom he must always care for and who took terrible advantage, and one sister older, who was stronger . . . and always right.

"I just want my net," he said in a strained voice, though clearly he also wanted a little revenge.

"Promise!" Lani's weight settled heavily upon his legs.

After more futile struggle, seeing that he would be a prisoner until he did agree, Mark surrendered. "Okay. But someday I'm going to be bigger than you."

"We'll see," Lani said smugly. "I always drink *all* my milk."

"Aaagghh!" Mark gurgled in his throat.

He was a very nice boy and an exceptional brother, but at times his patience was stretched to the limit. And when that occurred, he made strange noises.

Lani helped him to his feet, and they mounted the rest of the steps side by side.

The upstairs of the summer cottage was divided

into a bathroom, two small bedrooms, and one *very* small room over the stairs. In one of the small bedrooms there was a creaky double bed that was nearly as big as the room itself, and Mother and Father shared this space. Lani and Mark shared the other small bedroom, which held two twin beds and a dresser. Laurie had been given the very small room over the staircase since she sometimes took afternoon naps and needed quiet space to herself.

Lani and Mark arrived before the closed door to the very small bedroom and knocked.

"Who's there?" Laurie asked in a singsong voice, knowing full well who was there.

Lani rolled her eyes at Mark. "Us. Let us in." She added the word *please,* but not very politely.

The instant the door cracked open, Mark and Lani crowded inside.

"Where's my net?" Mark growled.

"You shouldn't have run off like that," Lani scolded.

Laurie tossed her curls. "I didn't want you to see what I caught. It's special."

"If it's so special, you'd show us," Mark grumbled.

"Not if it's a big secret," Laurie said with a smug smile.

"In other words," Mark said in the superior fashion he adopted when talking down to his smaller sister, "it's a common old sulphur. So give me back my net."

Ordinarily when Mark played the know-it-all, it

drove Laurie to do something childish such as sticking out her tongue or making a face. Now, however, she simply walked to the corner where the net stood.

Lani and Mark looked at each other, then peered about the room, trying to spot the something special that was making Laurie act so adult.

"What's so special about this butterfly?" Lani asked as Laurie handed the net to Mark.

Laurie shook her head, her blond curls flying, and said nothing. This was also very peculiar behavior, for Laurie usually said a great deal even when she had nothing worth saying.

The two older children moved slowly from the room, Mark in front, looking over his net for holes, Lani lagging behind. Lani turned her head and saw that Laurie had closed her door to a slit but was watching after her in a most secretive manner.

Laurie suddenly widened the door opening and curled a finger at Lani, beckoning her back.

"Are you going to tell me what it is?" Lani asked, her face bright with interest.

"It *glows*," Laurie whispered mysteriously, and quickly shut the door.

2.
THE SECRET IN THE BOTTLE

IT was close to midnight when the family returned from the drive-in theater. Father carried Laurie, who had fallen asleep ten minutes after the movie began, up to bed while Mother herded Mark and Lani toward the bathroom.

The two older children dabbed at their faces with damp washcloths, brushed only half the teeth they should have, kissed Mother good night, and fell into bed exhausted. No sooner were they on that floaty side of almost being asleep, than Laurie padded barefoot into their room.

"Mark, Lani, my butterfly is glowing. It's keeping me awake."

Mark mumbled, "It's not a butterfly, silly. It's a firefly."

Lani said through a yawn, "It's in a bottle, isn't it?"

At Laurie's "Uh-huh," she continued. "So put the bottle in a dresser drawer and close the drawer."

"I did, but the drawer doesn't shut all the way and now it's stuck open." Her speech became louder with each word.

A voice came from their parents' bedroom. "Laurie, is that you?"

"Yes, Mother."

"Why are you up at this hour?"

"It's her firefly — " Lani began.

"It's not a firefly," Laurie hissed.

" — its light is bothering her," Lani ended.

"Then let the poor creature go," Mother said.

"It's past midnight, Pumpkin," Father called. "Get to bed. Immediately."

Sighing, Mark sat up. "I'll turn it loose outside, Father."

"No," Laurie gasped loudly, "it's mine!"

Father said firmly, "Either put it downstairs or turn it loose. Mark, you and Lani go with her and make certain the lights are turned out before coming back upstairs. And shut our door," he added.

Laurie waited until Mark and Lani had pushed their covers aside and swung their feet to the floor before leading the way back down the hall toward the very small bedroom.

Lani snapped on the hallway light and closed her parents' door as they went. " 'Night."

" 'Night, good night," they answered. The double bed creaked as they settled down to sleep.

The hall light flooded Laurie's room. Only the corner where the dresser stood held shadows.

"Which drawer?" Lani asked.

"The bottom one," Laurie pointed.

The drawer was, indeed, pulled out. But neither of the older children could see a glow of any kind coming from it.

"Oh, Laurie," Mark said shortly, "you're just not sleepy because you slept through the movie, and now you're keeping everybody else awake."

"I am not, and it does too glow! I covered the jar with a towel."

"So why wake us up?" Mark groaned.

"Be quiet, you two. There's no point in arguing," Lani said, sounding very much like Mother. She knelt before the drawer. There was the dry squeak of wood rubbing against wood as she tugged at the drawer pulls. The drawer came open so suddenly, she fell back upon the floor. Laurie giggled. Losing her patience, Lani scrambled onto her knees, felt around for the towel, and jerked it off the jar.

The inside of the drawer was at once filled by a very definite glow.

"Oh!" gasped Lani. "How many fireflies have you got in that jar?"

"If you put fireflies in with the butterfly, the butter-

fly's wings will be damaged. You shouldn't keep a butterfly in a jar anyway," Mark scolded as he stooped beside Lani. "You should know better."

"There aren't any *fireflies*," Laurie insisted for what she felt was the hundredth time. She peered over their shoulders at the glowing jar. Then, losing interest, she stood back and turned in circles, watching the hem of her long cotton nightie swirl about her ankles in a pleasing fashion.

Lani leaned forward until her nose was only three inches from the bottle. "I can't make anything out. It's all sort of blurry inside."

Mark moved in closer for a clearer look. It was exactly as Lani said, all blurry inside. The center of the glow, however — the part where it was the brightest — seemed to be moving very rapidly within the bottle.

"This is really weird." Mark frowned. "Perhaps it's a new species. I think we should tell Father."

Lani picked up the jar and got to her feet, yawning. "Not tonight. C'mon, let's put it downstairs. He can look at it tomorrow."

"Tell him I caught it," Laurie said.

"We will," Lani promised over her shoulder as she led the way down the steps, the bottle held in front of her.

Mark's scientific curiosity was roused, however. He said, "If we put it in the refrigerator for ten minutes, the cold would slow down whatever it is that's moving and then we could see what it is."

"You can stay up if you want, but I'm going to bed," Lani said.

"Me, too," Laurie echoed.

It is doubtful the three sleepy children would have stayed downstairs for even ten minutes to examine the contents of the bottle, except that Laurie dropped a glass getting a drink. By the time they swept the floor and mopped up the spilled water, they were all wide awake and irritable with each other.

"I'm going to look at Laurie's jar," Mark said, opening the fridge. "It's been more than ten minutes."

The girls were crowded close beside him, determined that he should not see anything before they did themselves.

"Let me see first!" Laurie demanded, pushing against one side of Mark as he withdrew the bottle. "I caught it!"

"Wait your turn," Lani snapped, pushing against his other side.

"Take it easy, you two!" Mark held the bottle up over his head. "I'll put it on the dining room table where we can all see it at the same time."

Within the minute, they had the overhead light in the dining room turned on and were huddled around one corner of the table. Mark and Lani sat in chairs while Laurie stood between them, their entire attention riveted on the bottle.

The glass had fogged in the warmer air so they still could not see the thing in the bottle too clearly.

Lani said tentatively, "A chrysalis?" The thing didn't have the rounded peanut-shell look most chrysalides had before changing into a butterfly or moth, but she couldn't think what else it might be.

Mark shook his head without taking his eyes from it. "That stage comes *before* the butterfly."

"And it was moving around before," Laurie added.

They studied it in silence.

"That's odd," Mark said. "I don't see any antennae. All insects have antennae even if they're tiny. I'm sure it's a new species," he repeated, "or at least an unusual one." You could tell he wanted to wake Father and get his professional opinion.

Lani suggested, "Why don't we hammer airholes in the lid so it won't be so humid inside. Then we could see."

"That'd wake Them for sure," Mark said.

"We could go out on the lawn and punch the holes. Then They wouldn't hear."

In short order, Mark had located the hammer and ice pick, and the three children were outside on the damp night grass. The back porch light lit the area. Lani held the bottle while Mark tapped holes into the lid.

Laurie stayed close to them, hugging herself against the night chill, her eyes rolling toward the darker areas beneath the pine trees. Beyond the small stepped dam next to the cottage, a family of raccoons chittered to one another. And from the far end of the pond came loud splashing noises.

"Deer," Mark reassured his sisters.

After about a half dozen holes, Lani said impatiently, "That's enough," and they tramped back inside. They settled around the table as they had before.

A gasp from Laurie jerked Mark's and Lani's attention from the bottle. Laurie's chin rested on the table, and she had a direct view the other two lacked. "I — I saw a foot!"

"Silly!" Mark scoffed.

"I did, I did!" she said loudly.

"Shhh, you'll wake Them," Lani reminded her brother and sister.

Another gasp from Laurie made Lani and Mark glance quickly away from her toward the bottle. What they saw made them gasp, too.

3.
OCAVIA

INCREDIBLY, as the children watched, they saw one tiny foot, then another, appear at the end of the chrysalis-like thing. The whole form hunched forward and then straightened. Slowly, shiny, shivering wings unfolded until they extended about two and a half inches tall out from either side of a tiny form very much like that of a human. There were two arms and two legs and a torso, and a tiny face with two eyes and a nose and a mouth and two pointy ears. There was no hair on the little creature's head; instead, the back of the head rose to a crest. Two wings sprouted right where its shoulder blades should have been.

The three children froze like statues, their mouths open in astonishment.

The gaping mouths seemed to alarm the little creature. Its eyes widened, and then it was battering wildly against the sides of the jar. Its pale wings began to glow lilac, the color quickly deepening into a rich purple.

The children watched in helpless wonder.

Finally, the creature came to a panting standstill in the very center of the bottle. It put its hands upon its hips and bent at the waist, leaning forward as if to catch its breath. Then it righted itself and its mouth began to work furiously.

Lani gulped. "Its mouth is moving. I think it talks."

Mark leaned forward and put his ear against the air-holes he'd punched in the lid. He squeezed his eyes tightly shut so he could concentrate. All at once, he jerked his head up. "It talks! It talks English!"

Now, this was really splendid. After all, the tiny creature might have spoken French or Spanish or German or some other language. Since the children knew only English, they would never have known the creature was speaking real words; they would have thought it could only make mouth noises.

"What does she say? What does she say?" Laurie squealed.

"Shhh!" Lani commanded, and pointed upstairs.

Laurie whispered every bit as loudly, "What does she say? What does she say?"

"She said — " Mark stopped abruptly. "Hey, we don't know it's a she. It could be a he or an it."

"Oh, Mark!" Lani snapped. "Just tell us what she said."

"She said — " Mark blinked unhappily, looking from

26

Lani to Laurie and back at Lani — "she said, 'First you monsters try to freeze me to death, then you show your teeth like you want to eat me!' "

The children looked at one another, aghast. No one had ever called them monsters, and their feelings were hurt.

Laurie was the first to recuperate. "That's not very nice of her."

"No, it isn't. We're not cannibals, after all," Mark said.

"*She* doesn't know that," Lani said. "Here — " She pulled the bottle closer to her so she could talk through the lid. "Now, see here, we are *not* — "

"Stop it!" Mark ordered, grabbing at her arm. "Look at her."

The tiny creature had her hands over her ears and her eyes squeezed tight in pain.

"Maybe you should whisper," Mark suggested.

Lani nodded and tried again in a small whisper. "We are not cannibals and we are not monsters. We — "

"Her mouth is moving again," Laurie said. "Real fast."

Lani held her ear above the airholes. She shook her head. "I can't hear her."

"Let me." Mark reached for the jar.

Lani pulled it away. "No. It's my turn." She put her ear tightly against the airholes and held her breath. The little creature's shouts were faint, and Lani could

27

barely make them out. She lifted her head. "She demands that we set her free. She says she has certain inalienable rights."

"What's that mean?" Laurie wondered.

Lani tried hard to remember her American history class. "I think she means she has the right to vote and own property and worship as she pleases."

"And not be a slave," Mark added.

Laurie said, "We're not making her a slave."

"Maybe not," Lani said, "but we are keeping her a prisoner, and that's against the law."

A belligerent look crossed Mark's face. "What are you guys talking about anyway? We don't know that she's an American."

"I'll ask," Laurie said, and reached for the bottle. Lani moved it away. "Lani, it's my turn! 'Sides, I caught her!"

"Okay, okay. Only don't talk so loud."

Laurie whispered. "Are you an American? What's your name?" and glued her ear to the lid of the bottle. She frowned. "I can't hear."

"Try breathing with your mouth shut," Lani said.

Laurie clamped her lips together. "Oh!" she squeaked. She lifted her head, her eyes shining with wonder. "She said she's a *fairy*. Her name is Ocavia."

"O-what?" asked Lani and Mark together.

"Oh-cave-ee-ah." Laurie sounded out the syllables with great dignity. At the moment she felt rather proud, having a question asked of her that she could answer.

Laurie whispered into the bottle, "I didn't know there were fairies. Not really true fairies." She held her breath and listened intently, then sat upright, her cheeks blooming with blushes and her lower lip quivering.

"What'd she say?" Mark prompted.

"She's not very nice. She called me a dunderhead and said if she wasn't a fairy, what the deuce was she? She wants to talk to you." She grudgingly pushed the jar toward Mark.

Mark grinned and put his ear to the lid. To Lani and Laurie it seemed ever so long before he lifted his head and explained. "Since I made that remark about slavery, she said I should have the intelligence to understand that she is an American citizen by right of domain, whatever that is, and that she is being held prisoner against her will." He paused, then added, "And she didn't like my comment about her being an 'it.' She's a she and I'm an impertinent lout for questioning it."

Lani's lips firmed. Like it is in any close family, it is all very well for family members to call each other names on occason; it is *not* all right for outsiders to do so. Hearing Laurie called a dunderhead and Mark called an impertinent lout made her angry. "Give me the jar."

Feeling a bit despondent, Mark handed it over without an argument.

Lani whispered somewhat loudly, her lips brushing the metal lid. "Now, listen, you in there, fairies are supposed to be sweet little things, not name-callers. You are in no position to be snippy with us, so knock it off. Now, *you* say you're an American and are being held prisoner against your will. *I* say you are something we know nothing about, and we've every right to hold you prisoner until we do know what you are and . . . and" — she was running out of steam — "and then we'll decide what to do with you. I personally do not believe in fairies."

Lani looked triumphantly at Mark and Laurie, and then put her ear to the lid. She repeated the little creature's reply to the others:

"You accepted the fact . . . that I was a fairy the moment . . . I declared myself. Now, why . . . would you accept me for what I am . . . if you did *not* believe in fairies?"

"She's very logical," Mark said slowly. "I think we should wake Mother and Father and tell them about this."

Inside the jar, Ocavia suddenly began darting about. In seconds the three children were staring at a whirling purple glow.

"Why is she acting so crazy?" Lani asked.

"I don't think she wants us to tell Them about her," Mark decided.

Ocavia skidded to a stop and nodded vigorously.

Lani pressed her ear to the lid. "She says adults don't believe in fairies and she'll be poked and prodded and examined beyond endurance before they accept her reality. She'll . . . *evaporate* herself before she permits that."

"You mean kill herself?" Laurie quavered, her eyes rounding in horror.

"Let me talk to her." Mark took the jar. "If we tell our parents, will you kill yourself?" he asked.

Ocavia nodded once.

"What rot!" Lani said. "She's much too spunky to commit suicide. I think it's a trick to make us keep quiet about her until she can figure out how to get away."

Scowling, the fairy glared at Lani, her wings agitatedly twitching back and forth, their color turning a pink hue that swiftly changed to a bright red.

"This is really interesting," Mark said. "Her wings turn purple when she's afraid and red when she's angry. If we only knew what color they turned when she was lying, we wouldn't have to worry about her trying to trick us so she could escape."

Ocavia's mouth worked furiously.

Mark put his ear on the lid and listened. He sat up

and smiled crookedly at the other two. "Fairies, she says, unlike humans, are incapable of lying, as any fool should know from their white and gold wings."

"Humph!" snorted Lani. "Her wings change color every other minute. Besides, I know a girl at school with gold hair and white skin and she's the biggest liar I've ever met."

"Lani!" Laurie was shocked. "We're not supposed to talk bad about other people."

"It's the truth," Lani defended herself. "Anyway, I didn't mention the girl's name." Lani looked from her sister to her brother. "I'm not sure I believe all this. It's got to be some kind of trick or joke. But if it — if *she* is really real, what are we going to do with a fairy?"

"I could dress her in my doll clothes," Laurie said.

"The moment any one of us opens that lid, she'll fly away," Lani said wisely. "Besides, she's not a doll, and it wouldn't be fair to treat her like one. It would be like dressing up a cat or dog."

Mark mused, "I bet she knows an awful lot about all sorts of things. I think we should ask her questions until we can't think of any more. If it's true she can't lie, then her answers could be pretty important."

Ocavia's tiny black eyes darted from one child to the next as they spoke.

Lani said, "Look at her watching us. She's listening to every word we say."

"My decision is to tell Mother and Father," Mark

said. "I think you're right, Lani. I think she was bluffing about that evaporation business."

Tears sprang to Laurie's eyes. Being the youngest, she cried very easily. "But she'll kill herself. She'll 'vaporate."

Nodding vigorously, the fairy made wild beckoning gestures.

Mark said, "She wants to say something." He held his ear to the lid. Very quickly, his expression of concentration changed to one of wonder and then excitement.

"What is it?" Lani asked the instant he lifted his head.

"She said if we turn her loose, she'll grant us three wishes!"

Lani's eyes widened. "Is that three wishes apiece or one for each of us three?" she asked.

Mark listened again. "A total of three wishes. Any one of us can make all three of them, though she suggests it would be fairer if we each make only one."

"Anything, just *anything* we want?" Lani asked.

Inside the jar, Ocavia's head moved rapidly in yeses.

"Wow! Although" — Lani's eyes narrowed — "I can't see letting her go until *after* the three wishes are granted."

Laurie jumped up and down with excitement. "I'm going to wish for the most beautiful doll in the world."

"Now, that's really silly. You could wish for a

thousand dollars and then you could buy twenty dolls."

"Oh!" Laurie squealed. "Then I'll wish for a thousand dollars."

"Why not a hundred million?" said Mark.

Ocavia was motioning again. Mark listened. "She asks how you would explain having all that money. People would think you'd stolen it and you might be sent to — "

"Now, wait a minute here," Lani interrupted. "We haven't all agreed to this proposition. Let's discuss it first. What do you think, Mark?"

He frowned. "I'd really like to show her to Father."

Lani struggled to be patient. "But don't you see, you never can. Ocavia would evaporate herself before he could look inside the jar and then he'd think you were playing a joke on him, talking of fairies and showing him an empty jar."

"But we've never kept secrets, important secrets, from Father or Mother before," he argued, looking confused.

"Ocavia will *die* if you tell," Laurie wailed.

Lani shushed her sister, then spoke to Mark. "We could use one of the wishes for something that would help Father and Mother, something that they'd really like, then it wouldn't be so bad keeping Ocavia a secret."

"Like what?" Mark asked.

Laurie said brightly, "A new dress for Mother."

"Or a microscope for Father," Lani said.

Mark looked a little happier. "I guess you're right. I sure don't want to be responsible for a fairy dying."

Lani nodded. "Exactly. Then you're for taking the wishes and setting her free?"

"I suppose so," he said, but Lani could see he was still uncomfortable with the idea of keeping a secret from Them. "What about you?"

"It's okay with me," Lani answered. "Though it'll take me some time to figure out the best wish possible. What do you say, Laurie? Are you willing to let Ocavia go if she grants you a wish?"

Laurie's hands clenched together in front of her as she bounced up and down. "Yes, yes, yes!"

Lani reached for the jar.

"Wait a minute!" Mark said urgently. "If she can grant wishes, why doesn't she simply wish herself free?"

The girls looked at each other, wondering why they hadn't thought of that.

"Right!" said Lani. She looked crossly at the fairy. No one likes to be tricked, and she was beginning to think they were dealing with a very tricky fairy.

Ocavia folded her arms and stamped one tiny foot. Her mouth turned down in disgust. She beckoned and explained to Mark.

"She said," Mark repeated, "that fairies cannot make wishes for themselves, only for others. Everyone knows that." He raised his brows, his expression uncertain. "I didn't know that."

Lani shook her head. "I certainly never heard it before."

"Me neither," Laurie agreed.

"But it is logical," Mark said thoughtfully. "Otherwise they could wish to own the world."

"Or the whole universe," Lani pointed out.

"Or to be King Kong," Laurie chimed in.

"When you get right down to it," Lani said, "how do we *know* she can grant wishes?"

Ocavia crooked a finger and Mark bent low.

"She says make one and see."

"Can we wish for a pot of gold?" Laurie asked.

Mark told his sisters, "She says she's a fairy, not a leprechaun, but yes, we could wish for a pot of gold if we wanted, though having it would take a lot of explaining and it'd probably end up being taken away from us. Worse than that, most people would think we were thieves!"

The children glanced nervously at one another. They were realizing that the business of making wishes was not all that simple. They could get into all sorts of trouble if they didn't choose their wishes wisely.

"Let's start at the beginning," Lani said. "Are we agreed that we'll free Ocavia in exchange for a wish apiece?"

Laurie and Mark nodded.

"Then," Lani continued, "we've got to set up some rules so we can't be tricked. I'll do the negotiating."

Mark was too tired to argue, and Laurie admitted she didn't "know anything about 'gotiating."

It took a lot of hard listening on Lani's part — both her ears became very tender from pressing against the lid — but eventually the details of an agreement were hammered out. Ocavia would give them a maximum of three days to decide upon their wishes. During that time, she would remain in their possession, but she insisted upon a minimum of an hour of flight time in the fresh air each day.

"You can come with me and I'll fly along beside you. That way some dumb bird won't mistake me for a moth and gobble me up before I can explain." She had a very low opinion of birds. And toads. But most especially, bats. "The stories I could tell you about bats. Ugh!" She shuddered, the shudder passing along her body and out to the very tips of her wings.

"Oh, and by the way," she added, cocking an eyebrow, "wishing for more wishes is quite out of the question. That's cheating. And I can't grant wishes that would cause grief to another living thing."

The children, in turn, agreed that they would never, *ever* tell anyone about Ocavia, and that they would deliver one drop of honey per day and two drops of water, which was all the fairy said she required in the way of food.

Lani took a tired breath and whispered through the holes in the lid of the bottle. "Okay, we three agree to accept all your conditions and to free you as long as you, Ocavia, agree to grant us three wishes within the next three days. Are you" — she disliked using the word "agree" or "agreeable" again and it took some moments for her tired brain to come up with the word *promise* — "do you, Ocavia, promise to uphold your end of the bargain?"

She turned her head to listen, and it was an awful temptation to simply slump upon the lid and fall asleep, she was that tired. Laurie had already curled up in a chair and her eyes were closed, while Mark's head drooped upon the table.

The fairy cupped her hands about her mouth and yelled, "I, Ocavia, Holder and Protector of the Domain of Avia, do hereby agree. Now turn me loose!"

Lani blinked, her eyelids feeling as if there were sand beneath them. She slowly unscrewed the top of the bottle and politely turned it on its side so Ocavia could walk out if she so chose rather than fly.

But this really wasn't necessary because, faster than Lani could blink, Ocavia was gone in a golden flash.

4.
A FAIRY IN THE COTTAGE

LAURIE bounced into Lani and Mark's room and stopped expectantly between the two beds, looking first at her sleeping brother, then at her sleeping sister.

"Hi, Mark. Hi, Lani," she said brightly.

Mark groaned and cracked one eye open. "Don't you ever sleep, Laurie?" He rolled over to face the wall.

"It's late," Laurie said. "Mother asked me to see if you were awake. Lani" — Laurie pulled down her sister's summer blanket and whispered in her ear — "where is she?"

"Go away, Laurie," Lani mumbled sleepily. She pulled up her blanket to cover her ear and snuggled her shoulder deeper into her pillow. She was having such a lovely dream about a fairy.

Trundle trundle bang, trundle trundle bang . . .

Laurie was checking the drawers of the dresser that

stood between the two beds. "What did you do with her?" she asked. "Where's Ocavia?"

"Ocavia?" Lani's eyes flew open. It wasn't a dream! She pushed herself up on one elbow, her glance searching the room. Then, hanging in a fold of billowing curtain, a bright spot of white and yellow caught her attention. It looked just like a butterfly, but —

"Um, Ocavia, is that you?" she asked, knowing she was going to feel very silly if indeed it was a butterfly.

The tiny fairy flapped her wings and flew toward her.

Lani gulped and quickly sat up straight. "You stayed! I thought you'd tricked us, I thought — " She held out her hand and Ocavia landed on her palm.

The fairy placed her hands on her hips, her mouth working in an angry fashion. Even when Ocavia was in the jar and the jar was acting as an echo chamber, it had been difficult to make out her words. Now, out in the open, it was impossible.

Lani said, "I'll hold you up to my ear." Her breath battered against Ocavia's wings, and the fairy flung one arm across her forehead as she fought against the windstorm. "Sorry," Lani apologized, very carefully speaking off to one side in the tiniest of whispers.

By this time, Mark had launched himself from bed and now he and Laurie stood close beside Lani, watching Ocavia with rounded eyes. Lani tossed her brown hair away from one ear and held Ocavia next to it.

Plainly, Ocavia was speaking, and in a very agitated manner, but the sounds she made were very much like those of a whining mosquito.

"Would you say that again louder, please," Lani asked. "I still can't hear you."

Laurie edged closer, unintentionally nudging Mark. He pushed her back. "Stop shoving!"

"I can't hear Ocavia." She pouted. She felt terribly left out of things, since she stood the farthest away. "I wish she could talk as loud as us."

"OF COURSE I'M HERE! A DEAL IS A DEAL!" a voice thundered in Lani's ear.

Lani jerked back and Ocavia went tumbling down almost to the coverlet before her wings flapped the air. She darted to the curtain and clung to it.

The same loud voice wailed, "Oh, good heavens! What have you monsters done to me! Listen to how *loud* my voice is! It's enough to make a creature deaf!"

"Laurie!" gasped Lani, her eyes flashing in outrage. "Now see what you've done!"

The monumental loss struck Mark. He turned on his younger sister, absolutely furious. "You silly! You've wasted one of the wishes!"

Laurie blinked and shrank back. "I just wanted to hear her — "

Before she could utter another word, Mark leapt

forward and clapped his hand over her mouth. He looked anxiously at the fairy. "Does that count as another wish?"

Ocavia shook her head. "No, you have to say loud enough for me to hear you, *I wish. I want* doesn't count." Her wings fluttered as a breeze billowed the curtain and threatened to dislodge her. "But just listen to you humans! Thinking only about yourselves, when here I am trapped with a voice like a foghorn! Now no one's going to want to play with me!"

Mark blinked. "You mean you have playmates?" He took his hand from Laurie's mouth.

"Of course I do. Doesn't everyone?"

"There are other fairies?" Lani asked.

Ocavia shouldered her wings forward and gave each a little stretch. "There are other rare creatures like myself, though personally I find elves much more companionable. Very down to earth, sensible beings, elves. Not nearly so flighty." She laughed at her pun, but no one else got it.

Laurie said, "I thought all fairies had long, golden hair."

Ocavia made a disgusted noise in her throat. "What nonsense! Hair would get all caught up in our wings or blind our eyes when we fly." She ran her hand over the crest at the back of her head. "This is far more becoming and a great deal tidier."

"Are there boy fairies?" Lani asked. She was approaching that age when the subject of boys was intriguing.

Ocavia flitted to the top of Lani's head. "Oh, my dear, let me tell you."

But before she could tell, Mother came into the room. The three children had been so fascinated by the fairy that they hadn't heard their mother's footstep on the stairs.

"What's keeping you kids?" She looked at them a bit crossly. "I've pancakes getting cold downstairs." She looked curiously around the room, a little frown between her brows. "I would have sworn I heard a strange voice coming from this room."

The children looked at one another with wide, innocent eyes.

"There's nobody here but us," Lani said. Then she yelped.

Now, everybody knows that you can tug at a bunch of hair and although it is not pleasant it is endurable. But when one single hair is pulled, it hurts like anything. But that is what Ocavia had done. She had yanked one single hair — it must have felt like a rope in her tiny hands — on the top of Lani's head.

Mother looked at her. "What's the matter, Lani? Oh, where did you get that lovely barrette? It looks just like a butterfly."

Mark and Laurie paled a bit as they stared at the top of Lani's head where Ocavia lay still, facedown, her wings stretched out.

"I found it — " The same hair was tugged again, not quite as hard, but the spot was tender now and Lani flinched. "It — it came from the woods."

"A lucky find." Mother frowned at her, puzzled by her peculiar behavior, then looked at Mark and Laurie. They gave her sickly smiles. "Yes. Very lucky," she said in a hesitant, suspicious manner. Then, briskly, she added, "Now, hurry up, all of you. You can make your beds and get dressed later. The morning is half gone."

As soon as they were alone again, Lani said sharply, "That hurt, Ocavia. Get off my head." Ocavia winged her way to the dresser and settled on top of a hairbrush. "Why did you pull my hair like that?"

"I can't abide liars," Ocavia hissed at her. "You humans are *not* the only ones in the room. And *you* did not find me, your sister did. Now, dress quickly so your mother won't be upset with you. Children must be obedient."

Mark rolled his eyes and muttered, "I don't think I'm going to like having a fairy around."

Ocavia stayed in the bedroom while the children ate their meal. Father had already eaten breakfast and was in the office in the barn, so there was nothing to distract Mother from the fact that the three children were abnormally quiet.

She brought her cup of tea to the table and sat staring at their lowered heads for some moments before saying, "You children are not very talkative this morning. Perhaps you got too tired going to the movie last night?"

"Oh, no! Oh, no!" the three spoke at once.

"We had a — a restless night, that's all," Lani explained. Mark and Laurie bobbed their heads in agreement.

"After Laurie woke us, we couldn't get back to sleep for hours," Mark added, which was true enough.

"I broke a glass," Laurie confessed.

Mother smiled at her. She had noticed pieces of glass in the trash. "Accidents happen, Pumpkin, though I'm glad you told me. I thought," she said, changing the subject, "I'd drive into town to shop. Does anyone want to come with me?"

Ordinarily, all three would have chimed in with eager yesses. But with Ocavia waiting for them upstairs, even a drive into town and the possibility of some small treat — like a candy bar to divide among them or bubble gum — could not entice them away from the cottage.

Since Mother planned to be away from the house during the noon meal, she instructed Lani to make sandwiches for everyone's lunch and told Mark to clean up afterward and put out the trash. Laurie's job for the day was to dust the tops of the living room furniture while lunch was being prepared.

Mother kissed each of them and they stood on the front stoop and waved good-bye as she drove off down the road. She was scarcely out of their sight before the three of them were racing up the stairs to see Ocavia.

"Goodness, it takes you humans a long time to eat," her big voice greeted them as they burst into the room. She sat upon the top of Lani's headboard, one knee crossed and a leg swinging impatiently.

It was still very strange to have such a large voice coming from such a tiny creature, and the children could not help but giggle. Lani and Mark were already beginning to think that perhaps Laurie's unintentional wish was not such a bad choice after all, since now they could easily hear every word Ocavia uttered. Though they were pleased they hadn't used up their own wishes.

Mark carefully closed the door behind them, and all three settled upon Lani's bed, staring eagerly at the tiny little form atop the headboard.

"Well, where's my honey and water?" Ocavia demanded.

"Couldn't we talk a little first?" Laurie pleaded.

"Indeed not!" snapped Ocavia, and the children groaned. "Now, listen here! As long as I'm compelled by my word of honor to remain with you, I expect you to honor your end of the bargain. You promised me honey and water, and a deal is a deal. I'm famished. I need nourishment."

"Laurie dear," Lani said, turning to put a coaxing hand on her shoulder, "why don't you get the honey."

Laurie shrugged the hand away. "I'll miss something."

"Don't look at me," Mark said. "I don't want to leave any more than Laurie."

"I am not going by myself," Lani said flatly.

Ocavia shot up into the air and hovered over them, her fluttering wings beginning to pinken. "*Some*body go! Or do you want to call the whole thing off and let me go about my business?"

It was quickly decided that all three would prepare Ocavia's breakfast. Working together in the kitchen, they were soon back upstairs carrying a saucer with a single dollop of honey in its center, a cup of water, and — Laurie's idea — a piece of pancake folded in a napkin. They spread the fairy feast on top of the dresser and watched Ocavia dart down beside it to land gracefully on her toes, her wings tinged a peaceful blue.

She rocked back on her feet. "Good heavens! From privation to profligacy."

The children looked at one another, wondering for a

moment if she was speaking a foreign language. "What does that mean?" Lani asked.

Ocavia wagged her head back and forth. Clearly, she did not think much of their education. "It means first I was deprived of food and water and now I'm provided with an extravagant overabundance. Why, there's enough here to feed a ring of fairies."

"You could say thank you," Lani said with a sniff.

In his eagerness to satisfy his scientific curiosity, Mark interrupted before Ocavia could respond. "How many fairies are in a ring?"

Ocavia turned toward Lani. "Did you, any of you, say thank you for receiving a wish? We have a business deal here and mutual appreciation should be understood." She faced Mark. "A ring of fairies requires a minimum of twelve. Now, I would like to dine in peace."

While the children were in the kitchen, they had been wondering how Ocavia could eat without getting

her wings all sticky and stuck together by the honey. And how she might drink without drowning.

The fairy managed both with the utmost dignity and grace, hovering first above the honey and then above the cup of water, her hands going back and forth between the honey and the water and her mouth so fast that all that was visible was a blur.

"Ahhh!" She sat on the handle of the cup and contentedly rubbed her stomach, her wings gently moving to help her maintain balance. "I feel ever so much better. Though a bath *would* be refreshing," she hinted, glancing at them from the corners of her eyes.

"Like a birdbath?" Mark suggested. "There's one outside."

"Bathe with birds? How idiotic. I'd be some dumb bird's morning snack before you could blink."

Laurie motioned. "You could use the cup."

"Or we could go to the pond," Lani said.

Ocavia zoomed a foot up in the air and hovered, her wings a blur. A pleasant smile widened her mouth. "The pond! The very thing! A bath with you all standing guard so I wouldn't have to worry about being mistaken for a moth or butterfly and gobbled up."

With the prospect of watching the fairy bathe, the children dressed and zipped through their chores. In no time they were crowding through the front door of the cottage.

5.
THE QUEEN'S STORY

MARK led the way up the road a few dozen yards to where the trail around the pond began. He had a knapsack full of sandwiches on his back and a canteen of water on his hip. Lani and Laurie were fast on his heels. Ocavia fluttered close above them, keeping an eye out for birds. From time to time she lighted on Lani's head, since Lani was the tallest and the top of her head gave the best view.

It was a perfect day, warm and sunshiny with a light breeze to fan their cheeks — the sort of day that fills you with anticipation, when you want to be outside stretching your muscles with a walk in the woods, smelling the sweet scent of pine trees and listening to the cheerful sounds of nature or the happy talk of friends.

As the children turned toward the woods they saw a noisy group of Boy Scouts marching along the pond trail a distance ahead.

"Oh, bother!" Ocavia complained, and immediately settled upon Lani's hair and stretched out.

The children dragged their feet until the scouts were out of sight and sound.

"What I don't understand," Mark began, setting a faster pace, "is why no one has ever seen a fairy before."

Ocavia sat up. "Of course people have seen us. Many times. How else would you humans know fairies exist?"

"But no one's ever caught one before," he persisted.

"We don't know that, Mark," Lani pointed out. "Perhaps they were caught and evaporated themselves."

"Precisely," Ocavia said. "I never would have been captured except for that blasted storm. Imagine being whisked up by a strong wind and blown end over end miles and miles from your home like a — a scrap of paper. It was all very undignified, I can tell you. By the time the storm passed, I was too exhausted to travel. I crawled under a fern frond to catch forty winks, and the next thing I knew I was in a net."

"Why didn't you evaporate yourself when Laurie caught you?" Mark asked.

"Stubbornness, my people would say. I prefer to call it courage. Besides, I sniffed out right away that you, Laurie, were a kind child."

Laurie tossed her curls with pleasure and stumbled over a tree root. She quickly got her balance and hurried to catch up.

"Since," Ocavia continued, "you aren't the sort who pulls wings off butterflies or intentionally steps on ants, I decided to risk not evaporating and hoped to get free. I have very serious responsibilities to get back to at home, and" — her wings shivered with the thought — "evaporation is so *final*."

"Where's home?" Mark asked.

"Avia, of course."

"Where's that?"

The fairy rose to her feet atop Lani's head and turned in a slow circle. Looking somewhat confused, she sank back down. Her wings drooped as she said uncertainly, "Someplace off to the west, I think. Nothing looks familiar here."

"What do you do at home?" Mark asked.

"Why, protect my people and hold our territory."

"That's right!" Lani exclaimed. "When you made your promise about our wishes, you said you were the Protector and Holder of the Domain of Avia."

"Quite so. I am."

"Does that mean you're a queen?" Laurie asked in an awed voice.

"My dear," Ocavia said haughtily, "I am the ruler of Avia. What else could I be except a fairy queen?"

Lani asked, "Is there a fairy king?"

Ocavia blinked and her wings fluttered and turned blue with a pleasant thought. "Not at the moment. But soon, I think."

Mark said, "First you have to find your way home."

"Which," Ocavia said somewhat irritably, "I can't begin to do until you children make up your minds about the last two wishes. So I'd appreciate it if you'd concentrate on them and stop asking me questions."

She's getting cranky again, Lani thought. She reminded the fairy, "We have three days to decide. That was our agreement."

"Which doesn't mean you need take all that time," Ocavia snapped. "The number of our enemies increases every night. My place is there with my people."

Mark, who was still leading, fell back until he could see Ocavia. "What sort of enemies? Other fairies?"

"Of course not! Bats."

"Bats?"

"Hundreds of them. They've invaded our homeland and now boldly cruise the skies outside our cave. It's gotten so my people are reluctant to go out at night for fear of being gobbled up."

Laurie skipped ahead until she was nearly treading on Lani's heels. "But can't they tell you're fairies, not moths?" she asked.

"My dear, I'm beginning to think it doesn't matter a hill of mice to the dreadful creatures. A meal is a meal.

Of course, they pretend they can't tell the difference between us and moths, and are always so terribly sorry when we complain another of us is missing."

It was clear the topic of conversation was extremely upsetting to Ocavia. Her voice grew louder with each word and her wings turned pink. "Such squeaks of false innocence. Such hideous smiles of chagrin! It's enough to turn a stout stomach. And every day they get bolder, swooping past our entrances, sometimes lighting on the ledges outside to peer in."

"It sounds just horrible," Lani sympathized.

Suddenly, behind Ocavia, a large blue jay flew off a limb and darted down toward the brightly colored fairy, its bill open in preparation to swallow the tiny creature.

"Look out!" Mark cried.

Ocavia spun around on the spot. "How *dare* you!" she boomed angrily in her new human-sized voice, one fist shaking in the air before her face.

The astonished bird reacted as if it had run into a glass wall. Its wings furiously back-fanned the air; it veered to one side, swooping low to the ground before it gained altitude and reached a nearby tree. The blue jay turned about, its feathers ruffled, and edged side-wise along the branch, all the while loudly scolding Ocavia as if it were her own fault she'd almost been eaten.

The indignant bird was such a funny sight, Ocavia and the children could not help but laugh and clap their hands. And then, as it sometimes happens when a dangerous situation is avoided and everyone is relieved, they laughed all the harder until the noise of their happiness filled the woods.

"Well, my dears," Ocavia said, fluttering cheerfully in their faces, "I see there are certain advantages to having a large voice. In fact, it is probably more queenly. I suppose I can always whisper to my friends. I thank you, Mark, for the warning."

He grinned and made a courtly bow. "Your Majesty, my pleasure."

His courtesy pleased her, and Ocavia's wings glistened a regal golden hue.

"I thank you, Laurie, for using up your wish for my benefit." Laurie looked puzzled, so Ocavia explained. "Thank you for my big voice. And you, Lani, I will thank most heartily if you could locate a small backwater where I might bathe, and soon."

6.
THE PLAN

CUPPING a hand beneath Ocavia, Laurie lifted the dripping fairy out of the water.

Ocavia gave a shake like a dog does when coming out of the rain, then began to slowly fan her damp wings. "Lovely, absolutely lovely! My best swim ever!"

Keeping the hand holding Ocavia as steady as she could, which was difficult with the fairy's wings tickling her palm, Laurie climbed to her feet. "What can we do now?"

Lani suggested, "Why don't we walk on around the pond."

"We could hunt for the tree where the pileated woodpecker is feeding and eat lunch there," Mark said.

"I want to see the woodpecker," Laurie declared.

So it was decided. Still a bit on the damp side, Ocavia chose to ride atop Lani's head again. Her preference caused Laurie's lower lip to jut out. It was beginning to seem there was no sense of fairness in that fairy: Laurie thought that each of them should have a chance to carry her.

Sulking a bit and hanging her head, Laurie lagged behind on the trail. And so it was that she spied the small blue and red box off to one side of the trail in the weeds.

Curious, Laurie stepped aside and picked it up. It took her a second or two to push it open.

"Matches!" Laurie said with horror, the way you or I might say, "Snakes!"

Suddenly, everything Mother and Father had warned about matches and how tricky and dangerous they were loomed large in her mind. She stretched out her arm as far away from her body as possible, as if the wooden matches might flare up on their own, and wailed, "Lani! Mark!"

The others came hurrying back.

"What is it?" Mark asked, coming up.

"Matches!" Laurie said in a fearful whisper.

"One of the scouts must have dropped them," Lani said. "How careless! Put them back where you found them, Pumpkin. We're not supposed to have matches."

Ocavia was on her feet, hanging on to Lani's hair and peering down over her forehead. "I don't think that's a good idea. Some child who's not as cautious and wise as Laurie might discover them and play with them."

With Ocavia's praise, Laurie's chest puffed and all thoughts of the fairy's unfairness disappeared.

"You're right, Ocavia." Lani nodded. "We don't want any forest fires starting around here. Think of the cottage."

"Think of the animals," Mark said.

"Think of *Lion*," Laurie gasped, and tried to extend her arm even farther.

Mark said, reaching for the box, "I'll take them, Laurie. My pockets are big enough."

With the matches tucked safely in Mark's pocket, the little group continued along the trail.

Lani pointed. "Look, the Boy Scouts."

They paused to watch as the troop of eight came marching into sight across the pond. The scouts were singing and calling out to one another. They spied Mark and his sisters and waved.

Forgetting their displeasure with some careless boy among them, Lani and Laurie waved back. But Mark glowered, silently unhappy because they were making so much noise and scaring away every bird in the vicinity.

Some while later, Ocavia, who lay flat on her back, sunning herself, flopped onto her side and propped herself up on one elbow. She said thoughtfully, "It occurs to me that if you monsters could make up your minds — "

Lani abruptly came to a stop. "Please stop calling us monsters, Ocavia!" It seemed funny to be talking to the top of her head, and Lani ended a bit self-consciously, "It's not nice."

"We haven't been mean to you," Mark added, dropping back to join in the conversation.

"I brought you a pancake," Laurie reminded the fairy.

Ocavia fluttered up from Lani's head and hovered in front of them. She looked from one to another, clearly surprised. "I wasn't implying you're evil. If I thought that, I would have called you ogres. But look at the size of you — gigantic!"

"We're not *that* big," Laurie said.

"Compared to me, you are!"

Mark blinked. "Is that why you called us monsters when we first met, because of our size?"

"Well, why else?"

Lani giggled. "We thought it was because we kept you prisoner in a jar and put you in the refrigerator."

"Not a bit!" Ocavia laughed and danced through the air around them, in high spirits. "But speaking of last night, when are you going to make your final two wishes? As I told you before, I must return to Avia as quickly as possible."

Lani and Mark looked at each other. Neither had made a decision and, quite naturally, they didn't want to be rushed. Still, they wanted to be helpful, so they promised, "We'll think real hard about it, Ocavia."

They found the woodpecker's tree, a big old dead

elm with dozens and dozens of holes the bird's beak had pecked into it in search of insect larvae to eat. They sat on a log some yards away from the tree, where they would see the bird if it returned, though they knew that was unlikely after the singing scouts had trooped through the area.

Mark brought out the sandwiches from his knapsack and Laurie ate more than her share while he and Lani discussed possible wishes.

With a very full stomach, Laurie eased down off the log and fell asleep with her back leaning against it. Ocavia took it upon herself to stand guard over Laurie's open mouth and to shoo away insects who wandered near and might have flown inside.

"Have you ever tasted an insect?" she whispered to Mark and Lani.

They shook their heads.

She shuddered. "Disgusting flavor." Her wings turned a sickly green and she held a hand against her stomach. "I'm sorry I brought the subject up." She gave them a charming smile. "Well, have you dears decided on your wishes yet?"

Mark shook his head. "We need more time. A whole day hasn't passed yet, and you did give us three days to decide."

Totally forgetting Laurie's open mouth, the fairy shot up into the air five feet above them, her wings turning a color between pink and red. "I thought I made my situation crystal clear," she thundered, bringing Laurie instantly awake. "My people are being devoured, *devoured*, by those flying demons. There's an all-out war being waged against us, and my people need their queen to lead them into battle."

Lani gasped. "You never said there was a war on."

"I assumed you had the wit to understand that from what I told you!"

Laurie rubbed her eyes and blinked. "With guns and soldiers and things?"

"Oh, good heavens!" Ocavia spun up into the air in circles, going higher and higher until she was only a red dot in the sky.

Lani shook her head. "Really, this is not fair of her,"

she said quietly to Mark and Laurie. "She acts nice for a little while so we'll hurry up and decide. But like she said, a deal is a deal. I am not going to make up my mind until I'm good and ready."

Laurie squinted up at the red dot overhead. "But she must be awfully worried."

Mark looked at Lani. "Laurie's right. If we were in her place and something was threatening to eat Father and Mother, or we *thought* it was, we'd have a hard time being pleasant and polite with anyone who kept us from helping them."

"I suppose you're right," Lani admitted after some moments, "but I truly can't make up my mind what to wish for. And her being so pushy isn't helping."

Mark, who thought about things like this, asked, "I wonder if a fairy mile is the same as a human mile?"

"Why?"

"Well, Ocavia said she'd been blown miles and miles. If their miles are smaller than ours, Avia could be just over the next hill. If it is, we could go with her and help settle this matter of the bats. Then she wouldn't be so upset about our taking three full days to make the wishes."

"I don't want to fight bats!" Laurie said with a shiver.

"I didn't say *we* were going to fight them. I said we'd help settle the matter. I just can't believe bats really are bad."

Lani shook her head again. "Ocavia herself doesn't

know where Avia is except that it's off to the west." She dropped her head back and stared up at the fairy. "Maybe, though — " She cupped her hands around her mouth and shouted, "Ocavia, can you see your home from up there?"

"No!"

"Do you see anything familiar?"

There was a pause. "There's a tree on a far hill I might have seen before. I can't be sure."

"Come on down," Mark yelled. "We've got an idea."

Ocavia flitted down, but she wouldn't come near them. Her wings were still red, so the children knew she was nursing her anger. "What is it?" Her tone was sullen.

"We were thinking," Mark began, then paused to glance at Lani, who nodded, "that if Avia is not *too* far, we could go home with you and . . . well, if it's necessary, help you with your bat problem."

Ocavia stared from one to the other of the children, thinking it was some sort of twisted joke. Their serious faces convinced her otherwise. Her jaw dropped. "You really mean it, don't you?"

They nodded solemnly, Laurie a bit less surely than the other two. She wasn't keen on facing up to a bat, but she didn't want to be left out if there were " 'ventures" ahead.

"Oh, *oh, OH*!" Ocavia clapped her hands with joy. "What a magnanimous gesture!" Her eyes sparkled and her wings turned so shimmery gold, it hurt to look at her. "That would be wonderful! Marvelous! With you monsters aiding us, we can't help but win!"

Lani jerked her chin up and glowered at the fairy. "I asked you not to call us monsters. It is extremely un-kind and — and rude."

Ocavia lifted her wings in a flighty shrug. "I didn't mean to hurt your feelings, I simply forgot. But you are all so huge." She gave an excited, tinkling laugh. "That's it — I'll call you Huges," she said, and laughed so merrily, the children couldn't help but laugh with her.

The fairy's expansive happiness suddenly dimmed. "Oh, dear. Oh, dear me! I see a very big problem with your plan." She fluttered limply down upon the log, her expression sad. "Bats fly only at night."

Lani and Laurie looked to Mark for confirmation. He glumly nodded.

The children slumped on the log beside Ocavia, their chins in their hands, and tried to think of what to do.

"What if" — Lani straightened her backbone and the others glanced her way but without much hope — "what if we went with you to Avia now anyway? I mean, you saw a familiar tree while you were flying high up there, so your home can't be too far away." She jumped to her feet and stood before the others, her face brightening as her idea began to take more definite form. "It's only a little past noon. There's hours and hours before Mother comes home. Plenty of time to get to Avia and back before dinner. We could go and then we'd know where you lived. And when we've made up our minds about the wishes, we could come to Avia and tell you."

"Yeah!" Mark said, catching some of Lani's enthusiasm. He popped up to stand beside her in front of the fairy. "It would work, Ocavia. Maybe as we go along we'll even make up our minds about what we want to wish for and it'll all be settled before we get to Avia. Though" — he frowned — "I'd really like to see a fairyland."

"Me, too," Laurie joined in. "And then we wouldn't have to fight bats."

"Meanwhile," Lani hurried on, "you'd be home in Avia tonight to lead your people into battle."

As the children spoke, Ocavia's gray wings gradually grew lighter and lighter, changing to white as despair was replaced by hope, and then to yellow as hope was replaced by excited confidence. When Lani finished speaking, the fairy darted up above the log and burst into a thrilling, almost deafening cheer of victory.

"Surrender Avia, nay nay nay! Strive with Ocavia, ray ray ray! Victory is ours, hip-hip-hoo-raaay!"

None of the children had heard that particular cheer before, but it was simple enough for them to quickly pick up. In a fever of excitement they joined in, each trying to outshout the other.

Lani gestured off toward the west and cried out, "Lead the way! Ray ray ray!"

And stamping their feet and chanting wildly, the children fell in behind Ocavia as she flicked about to face west. Zigzagging in the air so she would not get too far ahead of them, the fairy led them off into the woods in the general direction of the Kingdom of Avia.

In all their excitement it never occurred to the children that after the dreaded battle with the bats that coming night, Ocavia might not be alive to grant them their last two wishes.

7.
THE SHADOWY THING IN THE WOODS

"I'M tired," Laurie complained. "And I want a drink."

Lani, without a pause in her stride or a glance over her shoulder, snapped, "I told you before, Laurie, the canteen is empty, so it's useless to keep asking for water. We don't have any."

Laurie wiped her sticky forehead with the back of her hand and stumbled to a halt. Keeping up with Lani and Mark was hard work for her. Her lower lip trembled and she thrust it out, feeling terribly sorry for herself.

"Can't we stop for a while?" she wailed at their retreating figures.

Hearing his younger sister's voice a distance behind, Mark paused to look back. He was the freshest of the three, being used to wandering with Father for hours uphill and down in hopes of spotting a bird new to their eyes.

Lani, doggedly following his footsteps but not really paying attention, collided with him. There were a few moments of confusion before they sorted themselves out and could give attention to their younger sister.

"What's wrong with her now?" Mark sighed.

The two older children stared back down the hill to where Laurie stood, shifting her weight from foot to foot in a listless swinging motion.

Lani called in a coaxing tone, "Come on, Pumpkin. Don't you want to see Ocavia's home?"

"I've got a big scratch," Laurie answered with a pout.

Mark squinted ahead. "We're going to lose sight of Ocavia if we don't keep moving."

Lani said quietly, "She'll come back for us. Laurie's tired and needs a break. I could use one, too. A five-minute rest won't make that much difference in when we get to Avia." Ignoring Mark's growl of impatience, Lani turned back, calling sympathetically, "Poor Pumpkin. Let's see."

Laurie waited until Lani was near, then twisted one knee to show a sizable red scratch on the back of her leg. Her eyes widened. Clearly, the injury looked much worse now than it had at first. She quavered, "I need a Band-Aid."

"It could use one." Lani nodded, peering at the long red mark. "But we don't have any with us."

"I thought I'd lost you." Ocavia's voice came from

above. She fluttered down from the tops of the trees to their level. "What's up?"

"The girls need to rest a few minutes," Mark explained. He followed after Lani, removing his knapsack, and sat Indian-style on the ground. His sisters followed his example, Laurie using the knapsack as a cushion to keep her big scratch from getting dirty. No one fussed at her for doing so since all the sandwiches were eaten and the knapsack was empty now.

With a prolonged heavy sigh, Ocavia drifted down to stand on the ground in front of them.

Lani asked her, "How far are we from that tree you spotted?"

"It's just over this hill and at the top of the next."

"Will it take us long to get there?"

The fairy kicked a fallen leaf. "At the rate you three have been dragging along, who knows?" she said scornfully.

"N-now, see here," Lani sputtered — she was hot and tired and scratched up, too — "we don't have wings so we can flit through the trees like you do. We have to bushwhack."

"Yeah," Mark grumbled. "This hike would be a lot easier if there was a trail we could follow."

"And water," Laurie added in a dry, cracky voice.

Ocavia was smart enough to recognize a near mutiny on her hands and to realize a change of attitude was necessary.

She forced a smile and said airily, "You want water? Why didn't you say so? There's a lovely little stream right over there with cool, clean — hey, watch out!" she roared as the children scrambled to their feet, nearly squashing her, and rushed off in the direction her finger pointed.

After drinking all the water they could hold, Mark filled the canteen while Lani used the tail end of her shirt to sponge Laurie's big scratch clean. Its improved appearance made Laurie feel more cheerful. It wasn't half as bad as it had looked, which is usually the nature of things, and a little sympathy often goes a long way toward sweetening someone's disposition.

Thoroughly refreshed, the children were once more ready to continue their adventure.

"Let's sing like the scouts," Laurie said, and off they went to the tune of a jolly marching song, Ocavia fluttering ahead and loudly singing with them.

They sang all the way to the top of the next hill, where the familiar tree stood to one side of a blackberry patch. The tempting sweet smell of the berries filled the warm, still air. Laurie stepped closer to the prickly thicket to pick a few and cram them into her mouth while Lani and Mark watched Ocavia fly to the uppermost branch of the tree.

Mark called, "Do you see Avia?"

Ocavia shaded her eyes with one hand and peered to the left, then straight ahead, and finally to the right.

"There!" she exclaimed. "There's Desperation Mountain! We're on the right track," she hollered down. "Sunshine Mountain and the Kingdom of Avia are situated directly behind."

"Behind" a mountain sounded very far away to Lani. "I don't know, guys," she said doubtfully, looking toward the lowering sun. "It's getting late. I think we'd better start back right now if we're going to make it home by dinnertime."

Mark said, "But we're so close to Avia. Ask Ocavia how long it will take now."

Ocavia, who was drifting down toward them, overheard the last remark. "How long will what take now?"

"The walk to Avia," Laurie mumbled around a mouthful of berries. "We have to be home for dinner."

"I could be there in fifteen minutes," Ocavia hedged.

"How long before *we* could be there," Lani persisted.

Now, fairies cannot lie, no matter how much they might wish they could in certain circumstances. So although this was one of those circumstances, Ocavia answered truthfully, "I'd estimate another three hours."

The children groaned.

"We should have started in the morning," Mark said.

"We didn't think about coming until after lunch," Lani reminded him.

"So now what do we do?"

"We've no choice except to go home. Right, Laurie?" Lani looked around when there was no response.

Laurie had wandered a few yards to one side and was staring down the slope of the hill. "Right, Laurie?"

She scampered back. "I saw something. Something big!"

"I meant," Mark said, "what do we do about Ocavia?"

Lani shrugged. "She comes with us."

Ocavia fluttered between them, her wings turning pink. "Now, wait just one minute! Before anyone goes deciding anything, let me remind you that I'm fifteen minutes from *my* home. I don't want to go back to yours."

"A deal is a deal," Lani quoted the fairy, "and you said you'd stay with us until we made our wishes."

"It's really big!" Laurie said, pushing against Lani's leg and looking back over her shoulder.

Lani sidestepped to catch her balance. "Cut it out, Laurie. We're trying to decide something here."

The fairy's wings hummed with agitation and grew red. She shook a finger under Lani's nose. "*You* said you'd see where I lived and *you* said you'd come back to Avia tomorrow or the next day to make your wishes."

Lani placed her hands on her hips and tapped her foot. "And *you* said" — Lani's heavy breath blew Ocavia backward — "we have to be obedient, which means we have to go home now if we're not to miss supper. And if we go home now, how can we return to Avia when we don't know where it is? I think you're just trying to get out of giving us our wishes!"

"So make them!" Ocavia said loudly.

"When we're good and ready!" Lani said just as loudly.

Mark looked from one to the other, blinking rapidly. "I'm sure I can find my way from home back to this tree. If Ocavia gave us a map of how to get to Avia from here, we could come back tomorrow."

"La-ni!" Laurie tugged at the hem of her sister's shorts. "It's going away."

Lani looked down, grateful for any interruption that might alter the touchy atmosphere between herself and Ocavia. "What's going away?"

"The big shadowy thing." Laurie had the others' chilled attention now. "It was right down there in those trees."

Mark squinted hard. "I don't see anything. What did it look like?"

"It was sort of hiding as it went, so I couldn't see the whole thing."

"Maybe it was a deer?" Lani asked hopefully.

"No. It was taller than that."

"Laurie, if you couldn't see it, how do you know how tall it was?"

"I don't know. I just know."

Lani caught Ocavia's eye. "You don't suppose it was

a" — she glanced at Laurie, then spelled — "B-e-a-r, do you?"

Although no one had ever mentioned bears living in the nature preserve, Lani couldn't think what something bigger than a deer moving through the woods could be *except* a bear.

"It's not fair to spell, Lani," her sister cried. She scowled and sat on the ground in a huff. "Mother told you not to do that to me."

Ocavia sniffed the air. "I don't think so, but I can't be sure. The wind isn't blowing toward us, so it wouldn't bring the animal's smell this way."

Mark glanced about, all at once a tad apprehensive himself. Without considering Laurie's feelings, he blurted out, "I didn't know there were any bears in these hills."

Laurie looked at them all with widening eyes. *"Bears?"* she squealed loudly. *"Bears?* Ocavia, are there bears around here? I thought they lived in jungles."

The fairy tilted her head toward Laurie. "Bears can live most anywhere they want except in deserts. But that doesn't mean that you actually saw a bear." She gave a phony tinkling laugh.

Her tricky answer led the older children to understand that that was undoubtedly exactly what Laurie had seen moving through the underbrush.

Lani looked nervously down the hill. "The shadowy thing you saw, Laurie, which way was it headed?"

"I don't know," she answered in a quavering voice, then pointed westward in the direction of Avia. "That way."

Ocavia said briskly, "Whatever it was, it's gone. Now, if one of you will find me a twig and you will all gather around, I'll draw a map on the ground of how to get to Avia."

It took some minutes for the children to calm their nerves and stop peering anxiously downhill into the underbrush. But eventually they found a proper-sized twig and crouched over Ocavia, watching as she sketched a quite decent map.

She explained. "And when you reach this point you'll be able to see the Carouthers place. It's an old tumble-down farmhouse on Desperation Mountain. Behind the house is a deserted barn. And that, my dears, is where the beastie bats live." She dropped the twig and dusted her hands before placing them on her hips. She lifted her head high, her wings turning a regal golden hue. "And tonight, that is where I, the Queen of Avia, will lead my brave people in an epic-making battle against the bats."

The children maintained a properly awed silence for half a minute before Lani pointed out, "But you haven't told us where Avia is. We should be starting for home right now, so we'd appreciate it if you'd get on with it."

Ocavia exploded up from the ground. She hovered

in the air above their heads, her wings a darkening red. "Can't you small-minded children think of anyone except yourselves?" she boomed. "Here I am, approaching a critical moment in fairy history, and all you can think about are your silly wishes!"

"They're not silly to us," Mark said, getting to his feet. And because he was upset at being called small-minded, he spoke of something that had been troubling him during their march. "And I don't think bats are bad animals. They have sort of ugly faces, but they can't help that. Father says they're useful, that we'd be up to our knees in mosquitoes if it weren't for bats."

Lani rocked to her feet and stood beside Mark, dusting off her knees. She felt a bit angry herself. It was very annoying of the fairy to be a friendly companion one moment and an indignant queen the next. "Maybe the bats were telling the truth when they said they ate one of you by mistake."

"One! More like a dozen!" shouted Ocavia. She glared at each child. "Just hours ago you three were willing to help fight them. Then it was," she mimicked, "oh, dearie me, it's dark at night when the bats are out and we must be home when it's dark. And now they're your cozy little friends who shouldn't be hurt or — "

Laurie let out a blood-curdling shriek. *"Eeeek!"*

The others looked at her rigid limbs and horror-stricken gaze, and turned their heads in the direction she stared.

So intent had Lani and Mark and Ocavia been on their argument that until Laurie's shriek none of them had noticed that a huge black bear had lumbered into the clearing where they stood, and was now headed their way, shuffling toward the berry patch just beyond them.

Reacting to Laurie's shriek, the startled bear reared upright onto its back feet, its paws batting the air as it gave a terrifying roar.

8.
SEPARATED

OCAVIA, every bit as surprised as Lani and Mark — and the bear — jumped exactly like a human would, only her jump took her up two feet higher in the air, where she hovered out of reach of those windmilling, awful paws. "Run, children, run!" she boomed in her human-sized voice.

"Run!" Lani yelled, her voice echoing Ocavia's. "Run, Mark! Run, Laurie!" And then, as she raced back down the hill they all had just trudged up, "Run, Ocavia!" which was a pretty silly thing to say to some-one who can fly, but not everyone thinks of the proper words to use in an emergency.

Mark bolted along the crest of the hill for several hundred feet before plunging out of sight down its western side.

Lani, who was racing away in the opposite direction, threw a terrified glance over her shoulder and saw that

Laurie was still standing in frozen horror directly in the path of the bear, who was still upon its hind legs, batting at the air in front of him as he shuffled forward.

"*Laurie!*" Lani screamed. Grabbing on to a tiny sapling, she swung about and began charging uphill — to do what, she had no idea except to somehow save her small sister from harm.

With Lani's scream, Laurie came to life. Her head fell back upon her shoulders as she stared up at the towering black form of the bear, her mouth agape. "Oooh," she breathed, and then she was fleeing downhill toward Lani.

As Laurie's churning legs brought her near, Lani caught her by the hand, and then the two girls were fleeing helter-skelter into the woods. They had no idea where they were running to. Their only thought was to get away from the bear, which they thought was directly behind and pursuing them. They ran until they hadn't the strength to run farther before they gave the first frightened glances over their shoulders.

The bear was nowhere in sight.

"Lani, I'm so scared," Laurie gasped, starting to cry.

"Shhh." Lani put a finger to her lips. She bent to whisper in Laurie's ear. "Me, too. I don't hear anything, so maybe we lost him. But we'd better hide until we know for sure."

She looked about and spied a fallen log. Motioning for Laurie to follow, Lani tiptoed around to its far side, and the two girls quietly eased down and sat on the ground.

The midafternoon sun played through the leaves and tree branches, and cast shafts of light where dust particles peacefully drifted. A tiny animal suddenly scuttled away through the dead vegetation on the forest floor, the slight noise tightening the girls' nerves almost to the screaming point.

They exchanged foolish grins.

"Lani, I want to go home now," Laurie whispered, her eyes glazed with tears.

Lani gave her sister's hand a sympathetic squeeze. "We can't, Pumpkin. Remember what Father always told us about not getting separated. We have to wait for Mark." She managed an encouraging half-smile. "He saw which way we ran, so he should be along any minute now."

Laurie stretched her neck as long as it would go to fearfully peer back over the top of the log. "But what if that bear comes first?"

Lani didn't answer.

After a while, Laurie edged over into Lani's lap. Lani put a protective arm about her little sister's shoulders and the two girls stared silently into the surrounding woods.

Meanwhile, Mark — who had run in the opposite direction until an overpowering ache in his side caused him to halt — was leaning against the trunk of a sugar maple, breathing heavily and pushing against the pain in his side. Standing there, catching his breath and hearing the silence of the woods, he began to think for the first time since he'd panicked at the sight of that lumbering bear. And what he thought was, *I acted like a silly jerk.*

(Mark was, remember, a woodsy boy who knew more about woodlands and animals than most other boys his age. And here he'd let himself be unthinkingly stampeded.)

"Black bears aren't like grizzlies," he said aloud, standing straight and kicking at the tree in chagrin. "That old bear was as scared from meeting up with us as we were from meeting up with him. He's probably miles away by now."

"Well, thank heavens someone has some sense!" came a voice from overhead.

Mark looked up to see Ocavia bouncing on the stem of a leaf, her wings stroking the air to hold her balance, their color a tranquil blue.

He said, a scowl in his voice as well as on his face, "Ocavia, don't act like you knew that bear wasn't going to eat us. You're the one who screamed 'Run!'"

"One of the ones," she corrected Mark in a cool voice, her eyebrows lifting.

"Where're Lani and Laurie?"

"Presumably, somewhere on the other side of the

hill. Precisely where, I don't know. I am not omniscient. I'd guess, however, at the rate they were traveling, that they're halfway home by now."

"They wouldn't go home without me," Mark stated emphatically. "We'd better go look for them. They're not a bit woodsy. They'll get lost."

Ocavia snorted. "There's no possible way for them to get lost. All they have to do is travel downhill. What I suggest," she coaxed, "is for me to quickly finish drawing my map so I can be on my way."

"You make it sound easy for them, but we climbed lots of hills. Once Lani and Laurie get to the bottom of this one, how will they know which hill to climb next? The least you can do is help me find them."

"Are you mad? There's no time! My people need my leadership now, tonight, if they're to win the war with the bats."

Mark gave her a grim look. "Lani and Laurie are more important than any old battle. Besides, I wish — " He caught himself. "Cancel that. I *think* you should reconsider that going-to-war business. If you'd only talk — "

"Oh, good heavens! Don't start telling me again how wonderful bats are. I'll hear none of it! Now, let's get on with the map so I can get out of here!"

"I don't want your old map! I want my sisters!"

"So wish for them."

"I'm not going to use up another wish."

Ocavia thrust her jaw forward, her eyes steely. "Ver-ry well! *Your* decision! Adios, amigo!"

In less time than it takes to tell it, the fairy queen was spinning upward into the sky.

"B-but," Mark sputtered, shielding his eyes against the setting sun as he watched her rise, "this isn't fair!"

"So make a wish," Ocavia's faint taunting voice floated down to him.

"Oh, aaagghh!" Mark cried, too frustrated to speak words. He looked around at the silent woods, then cupped his hands to his mouth and called. "Laaa-niii! Lau-reeee!"

There was no response. Again and again he called until he was hoarse. Then, dejected, he leaned his back against the maple and slid down its bumpy trunk to slump on the ground.

What a mess! The fairy queen gone and who knew where? And with Ocavia had gone all chance of getting the last two wishes fulfilled. What was making him feel even worse was that he'd been so greedy about his wish. He could have wished Lani and Laurie and himself safely home. But now it was too late. The fairy queen was gone, gone out of his hearing. And the three of them were separated in the woods with night coming on.

Mark swallowed and blinked back a tingling in his eyes. He looked toward the west and saw that only the merest edge of the sun still showed above the distant hills. In a few minutes even that would be gone and it would be night. Night . . . and the fairies would set out to battle the bats.

Battle the bats!

Mark sat up straighter. Ocavia's map! It showed where the old Carouthers barn was, where the battle was to take place!

He scrambled to his feet and began hurrying back uphill and along the crest toward Ocavia's familiar tree. If he could only reach those scratches on the ground before the light completely faded, he could see where that battle was to occur and go there. That was where Ocavia would be. That was where he would use the second wish to bring his sisters and himself safely home!

Every inch of Mark seemed to ache. His legs ached from the long hike, his shoulders and knees and hands hurt from the countless falls he'd taken in the dark, his head hurt from bumping into a thick branch, and his stomach ached from hunger. But he'd made it, he'd found the Carouthers farm.

Out from beneath the trees and standing in the over-grown farmyard, it was easier to see by starlight. He looked across the tumbledown ruin of a farmhouse at the shadowy outline of a huge old barn.

"Where the beastie bats live. Where the great battle is to take place," he muttered to himself. He wished

he'd had a chance to speak further with Ocavia about bats.

He settled himself on a cushy tussock of grass close to the remains of the farmhouse chimney. The toppled chimney gave a slight protection from a rising night breeze, and something to rest his back against as he watched the barn. After a bit of shivering, he remembered the box of matches in his pocket. No reason not to start a fire. It would help keep him warm and might act as a beacon if Lani and Laurie were anywhere near.

He cleared away the rubble of broken bricks from the old hearth, then pulled up handfuls of dried grass and piled them in the center of the hearth. With the first struck match, a spark caught and glowed in the dry grass. Mark bent to carefully blow on the ember, and was rewarded with a tiny flame. He fed it more grass, then scurried about collecting twigs. Once they were burning, he went farther afield to gather deadfalls from the forest and haul them back. Shortly, he had a large, merry fire dancing in the night.

He huddled his knees against his chest and sat as close to the fire's warmth as was safe. Slowly, weariness from his strenuous hike and the lateness of the hour caused his eyelids to droop, flutter, then close firmly as he sank into sleep.

9.
THE FAIRY CLOTH

"MOTHER and Father always told us," Lani puffed as she marched upward, dragging her sister by the hand, "that if we ever got separated, we were to meet at the last place where we all were together. That place is the top of this hill."

"But what if that bear is there instead of Mark?"

"Then we'll sneak away."

"I don't think I sneak so good. Besides, how will Mark find us if we're sneaking?"

Lani said tiredly, "You ask an awful lot of questions. Now, be quiet and lift your feet in case the bear *is* there."

Laurie said with a sob, "I want my mother and daddy."

Lani heaved a sigh and stopped and knelt in front of her sister. She wiped at the tear marks on Laurie's plump cheeks, making dirty smears. "Pumpkin, you've been a real brave girl so far. Don't go all criey on me now."

"But it's getting dark and I want to go home."

"So do I, but we have to find Mark first."

"He's probably already home." More tears flowed with another thought. "And eating dinner!"

Lani's stomach growled at the mention of dinner. "Look, we can't think of food and we can't think of home or even of Mother and Father until we find Mark. So come on!"

It was close to a half hour later. Lani was beginning to fear she'd somehow become turned around in their hike back up the mountain, when through an opening in the trees ahead she spotted the black silhouette of Ocavia's tree against the dark blue sky. Making shushing signs, she excitedly pointed out the tree to Laurie.

They moved forward as carefully as two tired girls could. The brush underfoot seemed to make a terrible amount of noise with each tiny step. Their hearts were pounding and they were clasping each other's hands so tightly that they hurt. They fully expected the bear to jump out in front of them at any moment.

"Why," said Lani in a normal voice, turning around and around when they reached the tree, "there's no one here."

"But where — "

"Laurie! If you ask another 'but' question, I think I'll

scream! I don't know where anyone is, but we're going to sit down and wait for Mark even if it takes all night."

"All night?" Laurie's loud wavering voice startled some overhead birds. In a flap of feathers which, in turn, startled the girls and sent them flying into each other's arms, the birds grumpily flew off.

Laurie giggled. "You were scared, Lani."

"No — yes." Lani giggled with her. "I was."

"Let's sing, can we?"

So they huddled under the tree and sang "Row Row Row Your Boat" and "Frère Jacques," and then sang them again.

"Laurie, look! A falling star!"

"Oh! It's so *big*."

It was. And the incredible thing was, it didn't appear to be falling toward earth, though it was coming closer. As it drew near, the girls could see that it wasn't one bit star-shaped or even round. It was triangular.

Intrigued, Lani stood up. "I've never ever seen anything like that before."

Laurie stood close beside her. "Do you think it'll hit us?"

"Hush." Lani cocked her head. "I hear something."

"Lan-eee. Laur-eee. Where are yooooo?" a distant voice called in a most spooky fashion.

"Oh, Lani, I'm scared." Laurie came so close, she stepped on Lani's feet.

"Get off," Lani said distractedly. "That's Ocavia's voice. I think that's her up there."

"Is she carrying a flashlight?"

"She's not big enough. Maybe it's a fairy spaceship of some kind."

The bright thing, whatever it was, was approaching the tree.

"Here!" Lani shouted. "We're down here."

"Ocavia! Ocavia!" Laurie screamed.

"We're down here under your tree," Lani yelled louder.

The eerie light began to curve downward toward the top of the tree they stood beneath.

"Girls! Found you at last!" Ocavia's familiar voice boomed with satisfaction.

Now, when one is lost and afraid, there is nothing lovelier than having someone who is worried about you find you. Even if nothing is settled, the lost feeling vanishes and, with it, the fear. Lani and Laurie both were so relieved to hear Ocavia's voice that even though they couldn't yet see her, they began jumping about and cheering as the light drew even with the top of the tree.

Then a very spectacular sight occurred. The light splintered into hundreds of pinpoints and each pinpoint filtered down through the branches of the tree. Only when the lights came to rest on the limbs immediately above the girls did Lani and Laurie see that the "star" had been composed of hundreds and hundreds of fairies. The area beneath the tree glowed with the golden light they created.

"Oh!" gasped Laurie with rounded eyes.

"Wow!" said Lani, smiling from ear to ear.

Ocavia ordered, "Put out a hand," and lightly settled upon Lani's palm. She strode back and forth, pleased by the girl's reception of her people and waiting for their attention to focus back on her.

Lani, always practical, was the first to speak. "Ocavia, aren't you at all concerned about being eaten by something?"

"Not when we're en masse and armed." The fairy patted at her hip.

Lani peered and saw that stuck through a tiny belt about Ocavia's waist was a long, slender thorn, almost a half inch, which the fairy obviously viewed as a sword. "Why are you carrying a weapon? I thought you said you couldn't harm anything living."

Ocavia lifted a finger. "I said I couldn't grant *wishes* that would cause grief to another living thing. We fairies may be small, but we do not lack for courage, and, of course, we are permitted to defend ourselves." She looked around at her glowing countrymen. "My people, this is Lani, and there stands Laurie, honest and truthful humans, staunch companions both."

Laurie dipped a curtsy. Lani nodded.

There was a hum as the fairies introduced them-

94

selves, though individual voices could not be distinguished. The girls, accustomed to Ocavia's loud voice, had forgotten how tiny fairy voices normally are.

Laurie finally found her own voice. She said softly, "They're very polite." She giggled. "And darling!"

An agreeable hum answered this statement.

"Are these all there are?" Lani asked.

"Oh, no, my dear. This is only part of our fighting force. The rest are guarding Avia."

"Have you already done battle with the bats?"

"It's still early. Plenty of time for that later. I felt compelled to make certain of your safety when my scouts reported seeing Mark at — "

"Mark?" Laurie squealed excitedly.

Several score of fairies zoomed upward, their hands covering their ears, their faces pinched in pain.

"Laurie!" Lani spat out. "Don't talk so loud!"

Ocavia stuck a finger in one ear and jiggled it up and down. "That was a bit shrill even for me."

"What were you saying about Mark?" Lani asked.

"There was a report of a fire on Desperation Mountain. When my scouts investigated, they saw a boy hunched before the hearth of the old Carouthers place. From their description, I knew it was Mark. He was tending a fire, to keep warm or cheery or perhaps to cook himself a meal. They didn't know."

"Mark's *eating*, Lani!"

"Hush, Laurie. Go on, Ocavia."

"When questioned, my scouts reported no sight of you girls. My conscience," she announced in a noble voice, "wouldn't permit my going to war until I knew you were safe."

"We're safe enough, but hungry and cold . . . and lost."

"And late for dinner," Laurie added. "I want my mother and father."

"Of course," Ocavia smiled almost slyly, "now that I'm here to hear, you could wish yourselves home."

"Oh, no, you don't," Lani said heatedly, ignoring Laurie's sudden look of eagerness. "We're in this predicament because of you, and you can get us out of it without our wasting wishes. Besides, if we suddenly appeared at home without Mark, what do you think Mother and Father would say to *me*? We're not going anywhere without Mark."

Ocavia gave her a beetle-browed look. "Don't speak to me," she whispered low, "in that rude manner in front of my people, or I shall leave you as I found you — lost!"

Practically nose to nose, the two females glared at each other, one with eyes a hundred times bigger than the other.

Laurie stepped closer. "Please don't you two fight now," she whispered. "We've got to get Mark."

Lani blinked first. It was true, now was not the time for another argument with the Queen of Avia. Lani managed a tight-lipped, "Yes, Your Highness," and even a bit of a nod.

There was a hum of approval from the closely watching fairies, and their wings glowed more brightly.

Ocavia lifted her head high. "My people, we will honor the desires of our human friends and reunite them with their brother."

"It'll take hours to walk there, and Laurie's tired," Lani said.

Laurie nudged her sister. "You are, too."

Ocavia lifted her arms in a gracious shrug and rose from Lani's hand. "What are fairies for except a little magic. Thonia, Lexia," she directed, "it will take both your companies. Ervania, have your squadron fly in support."

"Fly?" Lani gulped the question.

But no one replied. Little bodies were suddenly darting all over the place. On the ground before the girls, fairies began to unroll a tiny bundle of fabric. It looked a great deal like the cloth Mother used for dusting, only it wasn't see-through. Lani and Laurie watched in amazement as others flew down from the branches to aid as the unrolled cloth grew larger and still larger until it was the size of the hammock beside the cottage.

"Step in and sit down," Ocavia ordered the girls.

Trusting as always, Laurie immediately did as she was told. She squirmed about to give friendly smiles to the multitude of surrounding fairies holding on to the edge of the fabric.

"Lani, we're waiting," Ocavia said with forced patience.

Lani shook her head. "I don't know about this — "

"Get in!"

Quaking with apprehension, Lani stepped onto the flimsy-looking cloth and sat facing Laurie. "We're going to punch a hole in this thing as soon as they try to lift us," she grumbled. "This is ridiculous!"

"This is fun!" said Laurie.

"This is *magic*!" said Ocavia. She waved her arms and, while Lani flinched and Laurie giggled, hundreds upon hundreds of glowing wings fluttered so rapidly, they became bright blurs. The cloth with the girls upon it began to rise upward. A foot above the ground, it scooted sideways out from under the tree and then, with a swiftness that took the girls' breath away, rose upward until it was high above the tops of the trees.

Laurie rolled to one side and peered downward over the bodies of a half dozen hard-flying fairies.

"Laurie, *don't do that*." Lani held her stomach.

"I just wanted to see where we were."

Lani shut her eyes. "Can you see home?"

"No. Everything is black and my eyes are watering. I think I see a fire up ahead. Maybe that's where Mark is." She settled back and wiped the wind-tears from her face.

Lani swallowed hard and said weakly, "I sure hope so."

"You look."

"No, thank you. Maybe later."

Ocavia landed on Laurie's knee. "How are you girls doing?"

"Lani's scared," Laurie blurted out.

The fairy queen laughed with delight, which did nothing to improve Lani's morale. Then she said — and it was a surprise to Lani, for she felt Ocavia didn't really like her — "Not scared, surely. Merely unaccustomed to heights. Your sister is far too bold to be frightened of anything." She added with a mocking lift of her brows, "Even queens."

Lani, who had been hunched as low as possible, opened her eyes and sat a bit straighter at that unexpected compliment.

"Try looking up at the stars," Ocavia advised. "Once you're accustomed to seeing the stars while you're in motion, lower your eyes to the horizon. Work at it gradually, Lani. The only way to overcome a fear is to face it and go through it over and over until it becomes commonplace."

Ocavia waited until Lani was staring overhead without squinting or shutting her eyes, then lifted off Laurie's knee. "Girls, I must return to my command." With a wave, she flew off, one tiny pinpoint of light that was quickly lost among the millions of stars in the night sky.

"This *is* sort of neat," Lani murmured after a while.

With a carefree indifference to their height, Laurie shifted onto her hands and knees and peered down at the earth below. "We're getting close to the fire, but I can't see Mark."

Lani edged to one side and timidly stretched her neck to look at the ground. Ahead and far beneath them, a flickering red glow broke the solid blackness of the night.

"I think that's him," Lani said, pointing, "right there in front of the fire. He's hunched over, probably asleep, so he looks like a stump."

"Should we yell his name?" Laurie asked.

"He wouldn't hear, we're too high. Besides, we might startle the fairies and make them drop us."

Suddenly there was a brilliant flare-up as the strong night breeze whirled the ashes and coals in the fire-place, spinning them up and beyond the limits of the broken chimney.

"Oh, how pretty!" Laurie said gaily.

The scattered embers lifted from the fire showered back to earth, falling upon the dry grasses surrounding the tumbledown farmhouse. Without thinking about how high she was, Lani rose to her hands and knees so she could get a better view of the cascading sparks.

A horrible thought struck Lani, and she gasped aloud. "Quick, one of you fairies, fly ahead and tell Queen Ocavia we must hurry extra fast. Mark is in terrible danger."

"Lani," Laurie wailed, "what's happening?"

Laurie's sudden loud words battered against the fairies. The fabric lurched and tilted and, before the tiny creatures could bring it back onto an even keel, Lani and Laurie were tumbled together in a tangle of arms and legs.

"Ooof!"

"Ouch!"

"Stop kicking!"

"You're on my head."

There was a bit of pushing and shoving before the girls righted themselves and inched back to their original positions at opposite ends of the fairy cloth.

"Don't you understand?" Lani hissed the words. "If Mark *is* asleep, he won't be able to get away from the fires before they surround him. He'll be burned alive!"

10.
ANOTHER WISH

SOMETHING stung the side of Mark's calf. He roused himself and drowsily smacked at the area. Almost immediately, there was another stab of pain, this one on the anklebone beneath his right sock. He opened his eyes enough to peer toward the source of his discomfort, then jumped to his feet and jerked forward to slap at a red-hot ember burning a hole in his sock.

When he straightened, his eyes widened with horror.

All about him, small fires smoked and flamed, a strong breeze fanning their growth toward the old barn with every passing second. Mark looked from the fires back to the hearth in time to see a gust of wind stir and lift more embers into the night sky.

"Oh, no! What have I done!"

Poor Mark didn't know where to rush to first. He started for the nearest fire. In no time he had the flames of one tiny fire stamped out, but the others were growing by the second. He rushed to the next.

Overhead, there were great whooshing noises as hundreds of bats circled the area, squeaking piteously about the fires approaching their homes.

Mark never moved so fast or worked so hard in his young life. The instant one tiny spot of flames was stamped into smoking embers, he rushed to another. His sneakers became hot and began to smell of burned rubber.

He was wearily turning from extinguishing one fire toward another burning some yards away, when suddenly, overhead in the night sky, he saw two strange spots of light drawing near. The higher one, the brighter, was triangular. The other, a rough rectangle, seemed to be . . . *seemed to be carrying Lani's and Laurie's heads!*

Mark's jaw dropped and his eyes went wide.

Peering down over the edge of the magic cloth, Lani saw her brother surrounded by fire, his face blackened by smoke and his clothing singed. She did not have to pause to gather her courage. "Bold" Ocavia said she was, and bold she was indeed. She scrambled to her feet, took a wobbly step, and jumped out of the flying cloth just as it passed over Mark's head.

Whap!

Lani tumbled forward into Mark's arms, carrying them both backward and down into a heap.

"Bravo, Lani!" Ocavia's voice boomed from above.

"Hi, Mark, look at me!" Laurie sang out as the cloth passed and landed in the weeds beyond.

"Get off me, Lani!" Mark ordered the moment he caught his breath.

"That's a fine lot of thanks I get for coming to save your life," his sister scolded, rolling aside and scrambling to her feet. She jumped back from a hot spot she'd nearly rolled onto and wiped at her knees and elbows. "Now, where do you want me to start stamping out fires first?"

"Anywhere! Everywhere!" Mark wearily pushed himself up. "And thanks," he added as Lani instantly went to work.

Ocavia winged into view and landed on Mark's shoulder. "Whew." She wiped at her forehead with the back of one hand. "It's a tad on the heated side here. Almost hot enough to singe my wings. Good to see you, Mark."

"This is no time for socializing!" Lani snapped breathlessly as she danced about the edges of a fire, stamping here and there. "Do something, Ocavia. Help us!"

"I'm a bit petite to stamp out a fire, Lani! Be reasonable."

Laurie scampered up and flung her arms about Mark. "We were so worried! Eeek!" She hugged Mark tighter as a half dozen bats zoomed close overhead, stirring an angry hum from the fairies.

"Let go, Laurie!" Mark shrugged himself free and rushed to one side to stamp at the edge of a growing fire.

Forgetting everything Father had ever taught them about the creatures, Laurie hurried to Lani and huddled close, her arms over her hair. "Lani, help! There're bats all around!"

Ocavia did a circle in the air, scowling at her enemies. "That's because there are fires all around!"

Mark looked back at them, his brow creased in a worried frown. "And I caused them."

"Where are your fairies?" Lani asked Ocavia, peering about.

"In the grass, staying as dim as they can with those monsters out in force."

Just then, a black cloud of bats, perhaps fifty in number, swooped low, the one in front squeaking noisily.

Ocavia's glance shot upward and she thundered, "Did you hear that beast! Did you *hear* that beast!"

Lani looked upward in bewilderment. "All I heard were a bunch of squeaks."

"He had the audacity to suggest that we fairies started the fire simply to burn them out of barn and home!"

"Everything's going to burn if no one helps me," Mark cried, puffing as he rushed past them to another fire. There were sooty streaks on his face, and the whites of his eyes seemed enormous.

"Right!" Lani answered, and hurried to his side to help. "Ocavia, think of something!"

Left alone and shivering with fright, Laurie looked from the fires burning all around her, to the night sky filled with swooping bats. She was, remember, a very small girl who had been lost and scared by bears and bats, and was now hungry and tired. She was not lacking in spunk by any means, but her reserves of bravery were low. So her forgetfulness in what she did next is to be forgiven.

She said, her lower lip trembling, "I wish Mother were here just to give me a hug."

Instantly, Mother was standing there in the midst of the confusion, dressed exactly as she had been when she had left that morning to go shopping. Her arms were tightly wrapped about Laurie as she held her close, Laurie's curls tickling beneath her chin. She gave Laurie a squeeze and nuzzled her hair.

Then Mother's eyes opened wide. She looked up as a horde of angry bats flashed close above her head through the night sky. She looked to the right and saw Lani and Mark all singed and sooty-looking, stamping away furiously and impossibly at a multitude of weed fires. She looked to the left and saw a fluttering butterfly with a body like a minuscule human.

The butterfly thing smiled at her.

"Oh, my!" Mother's eyes rolled up in a faint, her arms relaxed, and Laurie slipped to the ground.

As instantly as she had appeared, Mother vanished. The hug was over.

Laurie looked peevishly at Ocavia. "I really didn't mean that."

"A wish is a wish." Ocavia shrugged. "Two down, one to go. And you must admit it was lovely to have Mother hugging you if even for only a moment."

Laurie nodded apprehensively. "But Lani and Mark are going to be *so mad*!"

11.
THE LAST WISH

LANI stood back from the flames and slapped her hands on her hips. She glared down at Laurie. "You did *what*?"

"I didn't mean to, really. The wish just sort of slipped out." Laurie blinked several times in her brother's direction. She nervously twisted back and forth, her arms swinging limply. "Would you tell Mark for me, Lani?"

With Laurie following timidly upon her heels, Lani marched to where Mark was still furiously battling the fires. "Do you know what *she*" — she flipped a thumb at Laurie — "did?" And then she told him.

Mark never stopped his desperate stamping for a moment. He said in a voice hoarse from smoke, "I don't care about silly things like wishes. The fires are growing and I can't put them out. The barn will catch

fire in another few minutes, and then the woods behind, and it'll be all my fault."

For a moment Lani stood very still. Then she turned
in a slow circle. For the first time, the awful reality of
the spreading fire and the terrible damage it would do
struck her. Mark was right. Worrying over a wasted
wish now was ridiculous and — and irresponsible.

She squared her shoulders. "Mark — *Mark*," she
tugged at his arm to get his attention, "we can use our
last wish to put out the fire."

For the first time since he woke to discover the fires,
the expression of worry faded from Mark's face.

"Ooh!" Laurie groaned her dismay.

"You are in no position to object, Laurie," Lani said
sharply. "You've already used up two of the wishes. It's
Mark's and my turn. What do you think, Mark?"

"I think we should." He nodded. "Yes. Definitely.
You do it."

Lani glanced about. "Now, where is that fairy?
Whenever you need her — "

"Right above you," Ocavia interrupted, drawing the
children's attention up, "and listening to every word.
It's a noble idea and quite a sacrifice, but it *would* save
the forest and with it the land of Avia. I would suggest,
however, that you wait until that horrible barn is
burned."

Lani grimaced. Sometimes the fairy queen could not

see beyond the end of her tiny nose. "And where, exactly, do you think the bats will go once they have no home of their own? Your cave in Avia, of course!"

"Hmm. You do have a point. All right. If you'll pardon the word, 'fire' away with your wish. I'm here to hear."

Mark was frowning. "Lani, wait a moment. Ocavia, tell the bats we'll save their barn if they'll agree to a meeting of bats and fairies and us."

Ocavia shook her head. "Such a meeting would be pointless. I don't think you understand the nature of bats."

Mark stubbornly set his jaw. "Okay, then — come on, Lani, Laurie, we're going home."

Lani started to protest, then caught Mark's wink. Playing along, she said, "Come on, Laurie!" and fell in beside Mark as he began to walk away. "I hope you can rebuild Avia, Ocavia," she called over her shoulder.

The fairy queen's voice boomed after them. "Pesky, disrespectful, cantankerous children!"

They kept walking. A slight luminescence on the ground showed where the fairies waited for their queen. The children turned aside to avoid stepping on them.

Ocavia suddenly flew in front of the children. She held up her hands. "All right, all right! I'll speak to the beasties. Wait here." She flew off. In no time she was back.

"They agreed, but only after I swore you really could save their home. They ask that you please hurry. A corner of the barn is already smoldering."

"Go ahead, Lani," Mark urged.

Instead of simply wishing for all the fires to go out — and of course they directly would have — Lani said, "I wish it would rain very hard on the fires and put them out, every single one."

Overhead, there was a tremendous clap of thunder. Big, fat raindrops splattered on the children's heads. The barn was the only building within miles with a roof, so without pause or consideration, everyone and every thing rushed toward it.

Spying a small side door to the barn, the children dashed through that, followed by a huge, bright clump of flying fairies, Ocavia at their head.

Inside the cavernous, empty building, everyone started talking at once as they shook the rain off. Ocavia directed her people to form a glowing circle and had the children sit in its center. The light from the fairies' fanning wings chased away all shadows.

Then, really heavy, heavy rain crashed upon the barn's tin roof, making a sound like ongoing thunder. All eyes looked up in time to see a flood of bats pouring through every broken board and hole. They

squeaked and flapped and settled and rose up and settled elsewhere to make room for the continuing tide of
incoming flyers until the space on every rafter was
filled and crowded.

"Lani," Laurie softly whimpered, her eyes round.

Indeed, it was almost terrifying to see so many bats
all at one time, and so near. Then the terrible aspect of
the bats was lost as, one by one, they adjusted themselves to hang head down from the rafters. Despite the
hundreds of glittering eyes turned their way, the children could not help but giggle, although somewhat
nervously.

Ocavia flew over to join the children, landing upon
the floor in front of them. "All right, Mark. You have
your meeting. You might as well begin whatever it is
you have in mind."

"How do I talk to — to them?" he gestured up.

"I'll translate."

Mark slowly rose to his feet. "My name," he yelled
because of the noise the rain was making, "is Mark,
and these are my sisters, Lani and Laurie. How do you
do."

Ocavia spoke to the bats in an astonishing series of
high-pitched squeaks and clicks, then turned to Mark.
"They say how do you do, and offer many thanks for
the rain which is extinguishing the fires."

Now that introductions were over, Mark was not at

all certain how to begin. So he did what Father, who was an excellent teacher, always did: he started with what he knew.

"I've been taught that you bats are helpful and necessary. You eat insects, hundreds and thousands of them every night."

"Quite true," Ocavia translated the bats' reply.

The thunder on the barn roof suddenly ended. A bat loosened its clutches and fell from a rafter, turning and swooping to squeeze through an opening. It disappeared, returning from the outside within seconds, squeaking with excitement.

Ocavia beamed at Mark. "He reports that all fires are out." She turned in a circle, speaking to her people. "Avia is saved! Avia is saved!"

"And the barn," Laurie piped up.

While the fairies glowed bright with happiness, a dozen or so bats joyfully streaked back and forth. It took a few minutes for everyone to settle down.

"Speak out, Mark," Ocavia directed.

"Well, if it weren't for you, our father says we humans would be up to our knees in mosquitoes."

"Also true."

Lani whispered, "Tell them about bat houses."

Mark slightly dipped his head to show he'd heard. "Our father has also told us that in Europe, a place a long way away from here — "

"We know about Europe."

"Anyway, in Europe, and now in America, humans build bat houses in their backyards. They want you bats to live close by because they know what a help you are to people."

"Quite so."

Mark smiled uncertainly, then looked down at Lani and whispered, "I don't know how to get to the part about them eating fairies."

Lani stood up and dusted off the seat of her pants. "It's this way, folks," she began in her direct manner. "You do a lot of good, but recently you've been eating fairies. Of course, it's probably by mistake." There were disgruntled noises from the fairies, which Ocavia quickly squelched. "But whether it's by mistake or not," Lani went on, "they're still just as eaten." She spoke in a low voice to Mark. "If that's okay, you take over."

He nodded and Lani sat down.

Mark thought for a moment, forming his argument. "You thanked me, us three, for ending the fires. But it really wasn't our doing alone. The fairy queen gave us three wishes. We used the last one to ask for rain. So you see, you owe the fairies, uh, something. Since you seem to mistake them for fireflies, I think the only fair solution is for you to agree not to eat anything in Avia that glows."

Now, no one likes to be told where and what they

can eat. Ear-splitting squeaks of indignation followed that suggestion so fast and furiously, Ocavia gave up trying to translate. Her wings turned a dangerous red, as did those of her people, and her hand moved to the thorn sword at her side.

Mark said sadly, "Maybe this meeting wasn't such a good idea after all. Now everyone's mad."

Lani stood. "Let me say something. Attention! Attention, please. We haven't finished." When it quieted, she went on. "You bat folks travel great distances. You can hunt fireflies in another valley. Don't be spiteful! And don't say you're after fireflies for our sake. We humans like fireflies. They make the nights cheerful. So by not nibbling at anything that glows, you'll be doing us a favor — and I'll remind you that you owe us one — as much as you'll keep the fairies from going to war against you."

Ocavia could hardly wait to finish translating Lani's words before she zoomed up a couple of feet above the ground, her thorn sword lifted. She shook it up at the bats.

Something like a cheer went up from the fairies, and now hundreds of thorn swords were lifted into the air by tiny hands, and threateningly waved.

Lani's last words, and the fairies' reaction, created the greatest commotion among the bats. It took some time for the bats' squeaks to quiet down enough for Ocavia to continue translating.

"We did not know the fairies intended war."

Lani glared up at the small, dark creatures. "Well, what do you expect if you keep gobbling away at them? They have a right to live, too, and they'll fight for that right if they have to."

Lani and Mark noticed that while the fairy hubbub was going on, a number of bats congregated on one side of the biggest rafter, clinging and crawling over and hanging on to one another.

Now, the congregation of bats separated and each took its place as their spokesman squeaked an announcement. Ocavia translated: "After due consideration, we bats will abide by Mark's suggestion. No longer will we hunt for fireflies — or otherwise — in the land of Avia. You have our solemn promise."

You can well imagine the joyous uproar that followed this statement. Forgetting her fear of bats, Laurie jumped up, and she and Lani and Mark threw their arms around one another and jumped about laughing and shouting. The barn was filled with hundreds of darting lights as fairies exploded into exhilarated flight, their jubilant humming louder even than the squeaks of the bats or the hurrahs of the children.

Ocavia fluttered about the children. "Well done, Mark! Well done, Lani!" Then, seeing Laurie's expectant expression, and because she was a wise fairy, she added, "And, Laurie! I never knew anyone who could sit so quietly during negotiations. Now there'll be no war, though I was" — she patted her sword and boasted — "rather looking forward to dispatching a dozen or so of the beasties."

Lani tried to look cross, though it was difficult because she was so happy with the outcome of the meeting. "Now, stop that kind of talk, Ocavia. Uh, Queen Ocavia," she amended when the fairy cocked a warning eyebrow at her.

"Yeah," Mark said, looking up at the multitude of bats crawling over and over one another in their own manner of celebrating. "Bats have feelings, too."

"True, but," said Ocavia with a mischievous giggle, "they don't speak English."

"Then they don't know that I think they're ugly?" Laurie whispered the question from behind her hand.

"Not a bit," Ocavia reassured her.

"Good!" She tugged on Lani's hand, yawning. "Lani, I want to go home now."

"Home," Mark echoed. He gave his sisters a worried look. "We're so far away, it'll take us hours to get home."

Lani shrugged. "So, we'll tell Mother and Father what happened, how we stopped the bat-fairy war."

"You'll tell them *what*?" Ocavia demanded in a loud voice, her hands on her hips and her wings turning pink.

"That we — " Lani began, then stopped. "Gosh, we can't explain! We promised you!"

"Precisely!" Ocavia nodded.

"So what *do* we say?" Mark asked.

"That's your problem!" snapped the fairy queen.

"Oh, Lani," Laurie suddenly wailed, "they're going to be so mad at us!"

Mark frowned. "Yeah, but how do we get home? We're miles away and it's black night out there."

"Ah," said Ocavia, "now, *there* I can help you!"

12.
HOME AND A
FUTURE PROMISE

DAWN was just breaking beyond the tops of the trees rimming Lincoln Pond when Lani and Mark and Laurie, surrounded by hundreds of fluttering fairies carrying them on the magic cloth, came drifting down to land beside the old hemlock tree where they'd had their picnic.

"Well, my dears," Ocavia said, flitting up to them as they clambered stiffly to their feet, "all's well that ends well, as I always say. Again, our thanks." She gave each a smile in turn. "And now it's time for me to return home with my people."

Lani eyed the exhausted fairies slumped upon the ground around the magic cloth, their wings drooping in the dirt. "They don't look like they can make it back to Avia."

Ocavia lifted her chin. "Nonsense! Thonia," she

boomed, "your company will repack the flying web. The rest of you, form up!"

Little bodies suddenly jolted into airborne action, weaving in and out until they found their places in a flying-A formation. Before the children had time even to think about thanking them for their ride home, Ocavia and her fairies were rapidly rising in the air in a flutter of wings.

"Wait!" Lani called. "Will we ever see you again?"

"Oh, please say yes," Laurie begged, her hands clasped in front of her.

"Anytime, my dears." The disappearing fairy queen's tinkling laughter drifted down. "Just come to Avia."

"We still don't know," Mark hollered, then ended quietly, "where Avia is." He looked at his sisters' unhappy faces. "That fairy!"

"Tricky." Lani nodded.

Laurie pouted. "She should have told us. Now we can't visit her."

"Right," Lani agreed. She braced her shoulders. "Well, we might as well go home and face the music."

"Are we going to sing?" Laurie asked brightly.

Lani giggled. "That's not what I meant, but why not?"

And that's how the children returned from their great adventure of settling a bat-fairy war, to the cottage on Lincoln Pond — marching in tune to a merry song.

"Good heavens! It's them!" a loud voice cried.

Lani and Mark and Laurie stopped at the edge of the lawn as a great crowd of people rushed toward them. Mother and Father, followed by the sheriff and his deputies, worked their way through the throng, and then there were countless hugs and kisses from their parents, and pats on the heads and shoulders from the villagers who had gathered to search for the missing children.

Once the initial fuss of the children's return died down a bit, however, and some of the milling crowd were returning to their cars to go home, the questions began.

"What happened? Where have you children been?"

"Well" — Lani took a deep breath, not knowing quite what she was going to say — "we went for a picnic. And then — "

"There was a bear and it scared us and we ran," Laurie piped up.

"And we got separated in the woods," Mark said. "I ran one way and Lani and Laurie ran another direction."

Lani said, "We ended up way beyond our boundaries. We're sorry."

Laurie smiled. "And I found matches and gave them to Mark and he — "

Mark gave her a nudge. "That was before we saw the bear."

"And he almost burned everything up!"

Mark said grimly, staring at the ground, "I started a fire to keep warm and it got out of control."

"My dream!" Mother gasped, looking at Father. "I told you I dreamed about the children fighting a fire." She hugged Lani and Laurie against her and gave Mark an encouraging nod. "Go on, honey."

"If it hadn't rained, I might have burned the whole woods down."

The sheriff exchanged disbelieving looks with Father. "It didn't rain last night, son. Just tell the truth."

Father frowned. "Mark, if you and your sisters went beyond your boundaries and became lost, simply say so."

Mark's face turned pink. He glared at the sheriff. "I *am* telling the truth."

"He is!" Lani cried. "There was a huge fire!"

"And the rain put it out," Laurie said smugly.

The sheriff stooped down in front of Laurie. "Where was the fire, honey?"

"In the woods." She smiled and bumped one hip back and forth against Mother's leg, happy now that she was the center of attention.

"Yes, but where in the woods? Can you tell me that?"

Lani said, "It was at the old Carouthers farm."

Laurie pouted. "I was going to tell him, Lani!"

The sheriff stood and tiredly nodded at his two deputies. "Might as well check it out as long as we're in the area." As the two men moved off toward their patrol car, he spoke quietly to the family. "I'm glad everything turned out all right, folks. But, you kids, don't go wandering again, do you hear me? A lot of people missed sleep and dinner searching for you."

"Yes, sir," said Mark and Lani in unison.

"I'm hungry," Laurie said suddenly.

"We haven't had anything to eat since lunch yesterday." Lani rubbed her hand over her empty stomach.

Mark cover his mouth and yawned. "Or been to sleep. I feel kind of dizzy."

With brief thanks and good-byes to the sheriff and a few lingering villagers, Mother and Father hustled Lani, Mark, and Laurie into the cottage. The children ate ravenously, and stumbled up to bed.

Late that afternoon the sheriff returned to the cottage. Mother and Father led him out onto the back porch to talk so as not to awaken the still-sleeping children.

"Honestly, I didn't believe your children's story," the sheriff began.

Mother said a bit stiffly, "They've been taught to tell the truth. They're good children."

"Yes, ma'am. Anyway, my deputies took a run out to the Carouthers place and sure enough there'd been several fires that almost got into the woods and nearly caught the old barn that's still standing." The sheriff paused to shake his head with wonder. "And

the ground was still spongy wet from an unbeliev-
ably heavy rainstorm that evidently touched only that
area. Yes, ma'am, those kids of yours are very for-
tunate."

The summer vacation was over. The family canoed
one last time about the pond, saying their good-byes to
the muskrats and the kingfishers. Then Father and
Mark pulled the canoe from the water and placed it
upside down on the back porch. Mother and Lani and
Laurie carried the remainder of their luggage outside.
While everyone else waited in the station wagon,
Mother made a final inspection of each room.

"Father," Lani asked, "can we come back to Lincoln
Pond next summer?"

With a picnic basket up front where Laurie usually
sat, all three children were sitting knee to knee in the
rear seat. Father turned to look at them. "Despite your
misadventure, you kids still like it here?"

"Oh, yes!" they answered in chorus.

He raised his brows in a doubtful manner while they
held their breaths, then smiled. "Your mother and I
like it, too. So yes, let's plan on a return visit."

"Yippee!" yelled Mark.

"Hurrah!" cried Lani.

Laurie squeezed his neck. "Oh, Father, I *love* you!"

"Okay, kids, settle down. Here comes Mother."

"Nothing left behind," she said to Father as she

slipped into the front seat. "The rooms look so barren without our things strewn about. And bigger."

"My hands look bigger," Lani said, staring at them. "I think we've all grown."

"We must have," Mark grumbled, shifting his shoulders, trying to gain an extra inch or two of space from his sisters who sat on either side of him. "There's no room."

"Maa-ark," Laurie said, pouting, "stop pushing!"

"Now, I want you children to sit quietly," Mother said in an annoyed tone. "We've a long drive ahead of us." She twisted to give each one of them the eagle eye, a warning glance that meant no nonsense! Her glance fastened on the top of Lani's head, and a strained look came into her eyes. "I see you're wearing that barrette you found."

A stilled silence fell upon the children. Lani started to raise her hand to feel for it, then stopped. She swallowed. "Mother, I don't think I should take it home. Could I put it back where I found it, please? It's not far, so it wouldn't take long."

Laurie scrambled to her knees and leaned on Mark's head to peer over at Lani. "Oh!"

"Get off, Laurie!" Mark ordered, then said, "Can I go with Lani?"

"Me, too," Laurie piped up.

Mother gave Lani a pleased smile. "That's very good of you, darling. I'm sure some unhappy little girl will come searching for it. And yes, all of you can go."

"No more than five minutes, kids," Father instructed. "What's this about a barrette?" he asked as the children piled from the car and raced off.

"Something Lani came across in the woods. It's quite unusual and beautiful, but it gives me the oddest feeling." She stared after the children. "I'm glad she didn't want to bring it home."

Out of sight of the station wagon, Lani and Mark and Laurie came to an abrupt halt.

"Ocavia!" Laurie squealed as the fairy rose from Lani's head and fluttered above them, her wings glowing gold.

"Well, my dears, you were leaving without saying good-bye?"

"We didn't know where to find you," Lani exclaimed, grinning broadly. "Gosh, it's good to see you. I was beginning to think we'd dreamed you up. How did you get on my head?"

Ocavia laughed merrily. "Why, through the open car window, of course."

"You never *did* show us Avia," Mark complained.

"Or tell us if ogres were real." Laurie hugged herself and shivered at the possibility.

"Or about leprechauns," Lani accused, "or how thorn swords work. Oh, there's so much we want to know."

"My goodness! Here I've come to say *adieu, adios, auf*

Wiedersehen, and good-bye, and all I get are complaints!" Ocavia scolded. But her wings remained cheerfully golden. "Of course, I would simply love to answer your questions, children," she said with questionable sincerity, "but your father said five minutes, and that's not nearly enough time to tell you anything except — "

"Yes . . . ?" they squealed eagerly.

"Enjoy being alive and learn everything you can!"

Throwing them kisses and laughing at their disappointed faces, the fairy queen twirled upward in spiraling circles, a disappearing, tantalizing spot of gold. "If only summers were lon-ger," she called in a fading voice.

"But we're coming back!" they hollered. "We promise!"

And they did go back. To the cottage. To Lincoln Pond. And, finally, to the land of Avia.

But that was another summer.

And that is another story.